THE DEVIL'S PLAYGROUND

Dr. Frank Conroy was a man in the wrong place at the wrong time. As medical officer for the Santa Fe Railroad, Conroy was well accustomed to the West's wild and colorful ways but he never figured that he'd ever be the object of a murder attempt.

A young girl's accident triggered an unlikely turn of events that placed him in the hands of the notorious Haskell gang deep in the Mojave Desert—with a price on his head and involvement in a kidnap. He had saved many lives in his time, but now in the Devil's Playground of a desert, it looked like he had met his match.

THE DEVIL'S PLAYGROUND

Cliff Farrell

This hardback edition 2004
by BBC Audiobooks Ltd
by arrangement with
Golden West Literary Agency

ISBN 1 4056 8002 4

British Library Cataloguing in Publication Data available.

Printed and bound in Great Britain by
Antony Rowe Ltd., Chippenham, Wiltshire

CHAPTER 1

Frank Conroy and Ramon Zapata alighted from the tool car as the work train groaned to a stop on the sidetrack at a construction camp called Pima Flat. They brushed dust and grit from their garb and dragged their luggage to the ground.

As usual, they were traveling light. Ramon Zapata's belongings were in a scuffed leather pouch of the kind that could be carried on horseback, or on one's back if the distasteful task of foot travel became necessary. His first chore was to loosen the drawstring on the pouch and pull from the interior a hand-tooled gun belt which supported a finely made holster containing a pearl-handled, silver-mounted six-shooter.

Frank Conroy watched with some disapproval as Ramon buckled on the weapon. "No shooting, my friend," he said. "I've got enough patients scattered along six hundred miles of track without you giving me more work to do."

Ramon smiled and wriggled the weighted holster into a position that suited him. "I'm told, Doctor, that this is a very tough camp, ramrodded by a person named Truck Eggers," he said. "I have heard that Eggers boasts that he has eaten the livers of men to whom he has taken a dislike."

"A crude way of telling me that the super at San Berdoo sent you along to ride herd on me in case I got myself into trouble I can't handle," Frank Conroy said.

His personal wardrobe was also carried in a bag. It was of heavy canvas, worn theadbare, and stained by campfire smoke and much travel on horseback and in railroad cars such as the one that had just landed him at Pima Flat. In addition to the possible bag he possessed a sturdy black case which also bore the scars of hard use. It was sizable, containing his surgical kit and instruments, along with a supply of drugs and bandages.

He looked around and sighed. "The old Mojave Desert," he said. "When the Creator decided to quit the job, this must have been the place He walked away from. Here it is, not yet the month of June, and it's hitting better than ninety in the shade right now, or I miss my guess. And blasted little shade in sight."

Pima Flat was a dreary maintenance camp in the middle of nowhere. The rails of the main line were twin bands of hot steel, glittering in the sun and stretching from skyline to skyline across a hostile land. The work train on which he and Ramon had deadheaded east from Barstow stood on a loop siding which served as a passing lane on the single-track line that extended from Salt Lake City to California terminals.

In addition to the tool car, the work train carried a flat loaded with rails, two gondolas piled with crossties, fish-plates, and kegs of spikes, and a bunk car which was bringing a fresh crew of laborers to this inhospitable camp. These arrivals were scrambling from the door of the hot bunk car and huddling together on the pathway that had been beaten alongside the track. They were gazing disconsolately at what was to be their home for months. They were all Chinese, clad in loose blouses, pantaloons, and sandals. Straw hats with cone-shaped crowns shaded their faces.

Frank Conroy shared their emptiness of spirit as he sized up the Pima Flat camp. A cooking and eating area had been set up beyond a blind spur on which stood two bunk cars and half a dozen empty flats and boxes. A tank car contained the only water available for many miles. A plank table and benches stood beneath a sheet-iron awning that at least shielded the rough table from the sun if not from the arid desert wind. A huge iron cookstove stood under an awning of its own, flanked by cupboards, boxes, and barrels. A rusty stovepipe elbowed above the awning, only a faint haze of smoke drifting from its mouth. There was no sign of the cook at this presupper hour, nor of anyone else in the camp.

A few items of coolie clothing flapped on a washline near the bunk cars. Sundown was at hand, but the work crew evidently was still out on the main line on foot or in handcars at the endless task of repair and reballast.

The implacable Mojave Desert surrounded the camp. A month earlier this land had been in bloom. Now the delicate primrose, the gorgeous verbena, the exquisite cactus flowers, were withered and gone, awaiting the far-distant awakening touch of the rare rains of some future spring.

Low, sterile hills and alkali flats dominated the foreground, studded with cholla and deerhorn cactus. A nearby dry wash bore a scant fringe of smoke trees and paloverde. Creosote brush fought with burroweed for survival on the flats. In all directions rose forbidding, slaglike ridges. To the north these uplifts were almost buried in great sand dunes. Few white men had ever gone into that labyrinth to the north in summer and returned. It was known as the Devil's Playground.

Frank's attention swung back to the camp which lay so bleak and silent. Ramon spoke. "Looks like everybody's away, amigo. Or dead."

Frank sniffed the air. "Or drunk. Bill Jennings told me at

Barstow that they had set up a moonshine still here and were making their own rotgut."

He turned to the group of coolies in the shade of the bunk car from which they had alighted. All their faces were as expressionless as though turned out by a single mold. Frank singled out one who was taller than the others and carried himself straighter. "You, there!" he called out. "What name you go by, boy?"

"If you're speaking to me," the Chinese said, "my name is William Ling."

He spoke perfect English, with challenge and a tinge of sarcasm. He was about Frank's own height and build, and apparently about the same age.

Frank cocked an eyebrow at him. "Seems like I've met you before," he said. "A hundred times."

"All chinks look alike, so they say," the coolie replied. "So do you Occidentals to us."

He *was* being insolent, also patronizing. Frank grinned, taking no offense. "Well, William Ling," he said, "quit being a wise guy. We're all in the same boat in this place. We work for the railroad, and the railroad expects to get its money's worth out of us. You will find bags of rice and boxes of tea in the tool car, along with casks of salt pork and a few other items. It's for you and your people. See to it that you don't waste it."

The insolence vanished from William Ling's dark brown eyes. "Thank you, Doctah," he said in his precise English.

"You know me?" Frank asked.

"By reputation only," William Ling said.

"Now, don't believe everything you hear, my friend," Frank said.

"On the contrary my people have told me that you have always treated them well," William Ling said.

Frank was embarrassed. "They were stringing you," he said. "Where did you learn to speak—"

"English?" William Ling interrupted him. "It happens that I was born in California. I am your countryman, although our skins are of a different hue. My father was brought over to work on the Western Pacific Railroad years ago when the transcontinental was being built. My mother stowed away on the ship, so as to remain with him. Chinese girls marry young, and bear children when very young. My parents live in San Francisco."

"Well I'll be damned!" Frank said. "A Native Son of California. Well, William, you and your friends get the grub and gear out and wait for orders. There must be a camp boss around here somewhere to tell you what to do."

William Ling beckoned to some of his companions and they hurried toward the tool car. "That one needs to be put in his place," Ramon said. "A smart-pants Chinaman. What are things coming to?"

"Just to think," Frank said. "He considers himself to be a human being just like you and me."

Ramon laughed. "That was one below the belt, amigo. This William Ling would be even more respectful if he knew that you bought the other items that you mentioned out of your own pocket to help out with the rice and salt pork—such as dried fish and water chestnuts and sweets. You always worry about these coolies out on the roadbed, and I have never seen you collect any kind of a fee for that extra care. How do you ever expect to get rich wasting your time on chinks? And on Mexicans like me?"

"It's a matter of laziness," Frank said. "Feed men well and they stay healthy. Healthy men, whether they're chinks, cholos or whites, on the end of a pick and shovel, mean less work for me."

He did not look the part of a doctor. He wore a clean, white cotton shirt, wrinkled from having been carried in his war bag, and loose cotton trousers, faded to a neutral hue by many washings. He had on heavy-soled brogans, for the short saddle boots, which he preferred, were not practical in this hot, loose desert soil. He was a lean six-footer, with short-cropped Indian-black hair and short sideburns. His skin was burned as dark as Ramon's by the weather and he could have been taken for a Mexican, except that his eyes were hazel gray. He had removed his weathered, wide-brimmed, flat-crowned straw hat to fan himself while he continued his inspection of Pima Flat. In contrast, Ramon was a dashing figure in slashed Spanish trousers, the slits laced with gold thread. His sateen shirt bore yellow braiding. He seemed slender and rather frail, but that was deceiving. He possessed the tempered strength of a Toledo blade, as many men had learned to their grief. He was the top trouble shooter and keeper-of-order in the raw, frontier settlements along the railroad. His father had been a Mexican revolutionist, and his mother the daughter of a hidalgo. Frank had been told that she had been a heart-stopping beauty.

A train whistle sounded. The westbound express was in sight, slowing, the engineer announcing that he was pulling into the loop siding back of the work train to lay over until the eastbound had passed.

Frank and Ramon, always fascinated by the might and the sound and fury of the iron horse, waited until the express had ground to a stop with a final blast from the steam boxes. The string consisted of a combination mail and baggage car, two seedy, alkali-coated day coaches, and two Pullmans that were equally whitened by the desert.

The tired faces of children and mothers were framed in the windows of the day coaches. The windows that had been closed to shut out the dust and grit of the journey were now being forced open in the hope of admitting a breath of cooler air to relieve the torpidity of the interiors. Men began disembarking from the coaches to stretch arms and legs. They were red-eyed, rumpled.

Among them Frank particularly noticed half a dozen or so who seemed to run to type—and that was hard formation. They wore the rough-and-ready denim and blue cotton shirts and hide boots common to the desert and to prospectors and miners, but their garb had a common fault. It was too new, too unsullied. In fact Frank was sure some of the costumes still had the wrinkles of store shelves. The wearers were scattered among the other passengers who were moving about in the shade of the cars, but Frank felt there was a bond of some sort between them. Furthermore they were armed, either with holstered pistols or rifles which two or three carried slung in their arms. Few or none of the other passengers were bothering to carry arms in this hot weather.

Other travelers, better dressed, not as travel-worn, were alighting from the Pullmans, helped down by white-jacketed porters. One of the first to disembark from the forward Pullman was a gray-templed, powerfully built man with an aggressive jaw and a stern mouth. He wore a tailor-made linen suit and an expensive Panama hat. He exuded the attitude of one who was accustomed to authority and expected attention.

And he was rewarded. The conductor came hurrying. "Is everything all right, Mr. Sloan?" he asked anxiously.

"Why are we laying over in this hellish place, and for how long?" the gray-templed man rumbled, making no attempt to keep his voice down. "That infernal sleeping car is a sweatbox, and it's not much better out here in the open."

"We're waiting for the eastbound," the conductor explained. "It should be along in fifteen minutes if it's on time."

"It better be," the big man said grimly.

"Is there anything I can do to make you and your folks more comfortable?" the conductor asked.

"Only get us to Berdoo as fast as possible," the big man snapped.

He turned and helped a middle-aged woman down from the steps of the Pullman. She was ample of figure, with pleasant features, but looked puffy and stuffy in fashionable mutton-legged sleeves, ruffled waist, and billowing skirt. Diamond rings glittered on her fingers. She spread an ivory fan and began using it vigorously. She gazed around at the bleak desert. "Oh, dear!" she sighed. "How long do we have to wait in this awful place, Henry?"

"Not too long, Harriet," the big man said.

The plump woman's glance rested on Frank and Ramon for an instant, and with disapproval. "I should hope not," she said.

The big man was offering a hand to a young woman who was also alighting from the Pullman, but his help was not needed. She skipped nimbly to the gravel and gazed around.

"Oh, it's beautiful, Aunt Harriet," she said. "So wild, so strange. I love the desert."

"Hola!" Ramon murmured to Frank. "A dove among the cactus. *Muy bonita!* Very, very pretty, and with a fine figure."

The girl was hatless. Her hair was a rich shade of dark, coppery gold, and obviously expensively cared for. She wore a seersucker skirt and white summery blouse that seemed to have fared far better than her aunt's costume during the train journey.

She was half-smiling, still fascinated by the desert. Her

glance passed over Frank and Ramon, appraised them briefly, and cast them aside, turning to a more interested look at the Chinese coolies who were unloading the stores of supplies. Then she examined the camp as though not wanting to miss any detail of the rough scene.

"It's just beautiful," she exclaimed.

"You must be out of your mind, Ellen," her aunt sniffed. "What's beautiful about it? I don't see anything but rock and cactus."

The conductor joined Frank and Ramon. His name was Sam Dobbs and they were well acquainted.

"Who's the nabob?" Frank asked.

"You mean you don't know him?" Dobbs said unbelievingly.

"Can't say I do," Frank said. "And I can't say I give a damn."

"What have you got your back humped about, Frank?" Sam Dobbs wanted to know. "What did Henry Sloan ever do to you?"

Frank shrugged. "So that's who he is? I might have known. I've heard of him, of course, and he's living up to a lot of things I've been told about him. So that's him in the flesh?"

"That's him all right. That's his widowed sister, Harriet. An' the gal is his daughter, Ellen. She's a real dish, ain't she?"

"Real attractive," Frank conceded. "And with all the earmarks of being a spoiled, conceited snob like her father. Too much money, too little in the way of brains."

He was annoyed with himself over his outburst, but the Sloans, and especially Ellen Sloan, with their sleek aura of wealth and power represented a way of life that he had never known, and, to tell the truth, it was an existence that he had never really envied or sought to attain. That was why he did not understand his sudden antagonism toward Henry Sloan and his kin.

"Steer clear of ol' Henry, Doc," Sam Dobbs advised. "Don't rub his fur the wrong way. He ain't got much use fer fellers in yore trade. Tried to kill a sawbones some years back."

"He tried to kill a doctor? Why?"

"Seems like he lost his wife an' a son who was only a boy. Blamed the doctor. That's all I know, except that Henry's said to be a man who's hell on wheels if he goes out to git you."

Frank knew Henry Sloan only by reputation, and he had never before heard about the man's opinion of his profession. Henry Sloan was said to be not only one of the wealthiest cattlemen in California but a political power who had his eyes set on the governor's chair.

"Why are they on your train, señor?" Ramon asked Dobbs.

"They're on their way home after bein' back East fer a spell, so I understand. New York, Washington, an' such places. The gal has been attendin' some of them high-toned finishin' schools where they teach you to hold the little finger at attention when yo're handlin' a teacup. They've got a big home in Berdoo, but they spend most of their time at Henry Sloan's ranch in the Verde Valley, at the foot of the Cleghorn Mountains. They say both places has got so many rooms in 'em, you kin git lost unless you have a guide. Me, I don't know. I never been invited."

Sam Dobbs, impressed by his own wit, uttered a braying guffaw that brought the attention of the slender Sloan girl back upon them. Frank felt that he and Dobbs and Ramon were being briefly appraised as probably capable of further weird antics. It again nettled him to realize that a girl he had never before seen would arouse his antagonism. Ellen

Sloan's new inspection ended quickly. She turned to her father, linked arms, and said something, smiling gaily.

Laughing, she cajoled her father into strolling along the foot-beaten path adjoining the sidetrack. Henry Sloan unbent. Smiling indulgently, he let her have her way in forcing him into unwanted exercise. He bent his head and gave his daughter a peck on the cheek.

"They say she's the only one who kin handle him," Sam Dobbs observed, watching the Sloans. "I've heard it wasn't always that way, though. Not till after he lost his son. The boy was only about eight when him an' his maw died o' fever. Henry was away at the time, up in the San Joaquin Valley where he runs a lot o' cattle. Didn't git back in time. Blamed the doctor. Might have had reason. The doc was a drunk an' a quack, so I understand. He lit out o' the country before Henry could find him. Since then his daughter has been the only thing in life he seems to have any use fer."

Frank picked up his war bag and medical case and headed for the camp beyond the spur track, with Ramon following him. Two tents stood near the cooking area, but there was still no sign of life about the place. His brogans grated in the coarse underfooting. The heat lay heavily on him. Each day, with the coming of summer, the weather would blaze down with increasing malevolence, and he would still be at its mercy—if not in this dismal place at another railroad camp or watering stop no more hospitable.

He had graduated from a medical school in Ohio after four years of struggle and privation, washing dishes in hash houses or taking on other menial chores to earn his board and to pay for his tuition.

The Spanish-American war had broken out at the time he had received his diploma, and he had served a long hitch in the Philippines with a hospital unit, gaining much surgical and practical medical experience, but finding that his principal battle was against the loneliness of young men who had dreamed of glory and romance in the tropics, and had found instead only monotony and boredom in a world far different from their expectations. He had been mustered out with little money and the best wishes of the Army, and the rank of captain.

He had one advantage, his medical degree, but he had soon discovered that it was not the key to ease and wealth. He had finally headed West and had wound up three years previously as a railroad doctor responsible for the well-being of workers along some seven hundred miles of right of way.

Ramon was at his heels as he walked to the tank car which brought Pima Flat its life-sustaining supply of water. The tanker was fitted with a valve to which was attached a short length of hose which served various purposes. At the moment the end of the hose lay idle in a large iron kettle, unwashed since having been used to cook food for the crew. The kettle was brimming with greasy water.

Nearby stood a wooden water barrel whose loose top was fitted with a wooden handle. A long-handled metal dipper hung from a nail on a post above the barrel, proclaiming that this was the camp drinking fount, the dipper available to all comers. The barrel stood in the last rays of the setting sun, and its contents was more than lukewarm.

Frank lifted the cover and peered into the depths of the barrel. It was half-filled with water, and he could see wrigglers moving in the murky liquid. Using the handle of the dipper, he probed the residue that had accumulated at the bottom of the barrel. It measured an inch or more. The drinking fount had not been cleaned in weeks or months.

He stepped back a pace, planted a foot against the barrel, and capsized it, sending a gush of water into the hot earth. The barrel kept rolling, bringing up with a thud against the cookstove.

"What the hell!" a thick voice exclaimed.

The head and shoulders of a man appeared above the plank mess table. He was balding, unshaven, and shirtless, but wore a grease-stained cook's apron over his bare chest. He was bleary-eyed and gave forth the aura of having imbibed cheap alcohol. He apparently had been stretched out asleep on the far side of the table. A fruit jar containing a yellowish liquid stood on the table.

Frank sniffed the contents of the jar. "Moonshine," he said. "Real rotgut."

He hurled the jar away, shattering it against the side of the tank car. The bleary-eyed man reared to his feet, aghast. "What in tophet do you think you're doin'?" he screeched.

"I take it you're the cook," Frank said.

"I sure am!" the man snarled. "An' I'm goin' to beat the whey out'n you, whoever you air."

"You had orders to strain and boil all water used for drinking and cooking in this camp," Frank said. "Also to see to it that ice is delivered regularly from Barstow and that the crew has decent cold water to drink when they come in. You don't seem to have taken the orders seriously. There's been dysentery and malaria among the crew here, according to what I was told at Barstow."

"Ice water, is it?" the man jeered. "Ice water fer them chinks? I got better things to do. I'm Brick Foley, the cook, an' I run my kitchen to suit myself."

"Not any longer," Frank said. "You're fired."

"Fired, am I?" the man panted and leaped upon the table, towering above Frank. "An' who are you to fire Brick Foley? I'm goin' to take you apart!" He was obviously poising to launch an attack on Frank.

Ramon spoke. "Easy, easy, Foley. It is best not to start trouble with my friend. He is—"

Brick Foley did not heed. He hurled himself in a flying leap at Frank, intending to bowl him over. He missed. Frank was there one instant and not there the next. Foley tried to seize him with desperately outstretched hands as he sailed through the air, but failed. He went sprawling on the ground with a thud that drove a grunt from his heavy lips. He was fat and gross of body. He was not hurt, but the wind had been knocked out of him.

Frank moved in, caught him by the straps of his cook's apron and the belt of his trousers, lifted him bodily, and walked toward the kettle of greasy water. "You need a bath in addition to other things," he gritted.

Foley began to kick and struggle and use strong language, but could not break free. "Blast you!" he panted. "Don't you—!"

He was no small man, but he found himself suspended like a huge insect, arms and legs flailing futilely. Frank swung him farther aloft and plunged him headfirst into the kettle. He leaped back to escape the wave of water that sloshed overboard.

Foley dragged himself, dripping, from the kettle, wheezing and coughing. "I'll beat you to a pulp," he gasped.

Ramon spoke again, his tone solicitous. "Do not do anything foolish, señor. This is Dr. Frank Conroy. He is the company doctor. He was also—"

Again Foley failed to heed. He rushed at Frank, fists clenched. Frank stepped back, parried a wild right that threw the angry cook off balance, leaving him wide open for the counterpunch. It came. A hard right. It drove Foley back on his heels, surprised shock in his face. Then he began to crumple. Frank moved in and eased him to the ground.

Ramon looked down at the recumbent cook and clucked his lips sympathetically. "I was trying to tell you that Dr. Conroy was the light heavyweight boxing champion of the American Army on the island of Luzon, my friend. But you would not listen."

"Pour some water on him," Frank said. "Turn on the hose. He'll come around in a minute or two."

"I would say he has seen water enough," Ramon said, bending over the drenched cook. "He is already awakening."

The passengers from the sidetracked train were staring. Also the coolies from the work train. Heads were jutting from open windows of the day coaches, eyes wide. Henry Sloan and his daughter were gazing also. However, Aunt Harriet, agitatedly flapping her fan in protest at such violence, was bustling toward the steps of the Pullman to remove herself from the scene.

Frank again sniffed the air. He followed what his nose told him. It led him to one of the shabby tents that were set up near the rim of the shallow dry wash. He lifted the closed flap of the tent and peered in.

"Here it is," he said to Ramon.

The tent housed a homemade moonshine still, with all the standard equipment—copper worm, small boiler, barrels containing fermenting mash, jugs and bottles on improvised shelves. The tent reeked of the project even though the equipment was not in operation at the moment. The boiler was cold, the ashes in its firebox were gray and feathery.

Frank swept the jars and jugs from the shelves and they crashed into shards. Some contained the potent moonshine, which formed puddles on the hard-packed earth. He kicked over the barrels, spilling the mash. He found a maul and used it to pound the brass worm into an unusable mass.

He sent the barrels rolling over the cutbank into the dry wash.

"Oh-oh!" Ramon said. "You have another visitor. Be alert. This is the one I told you about. The one who is said to dine on the livers of those he dislikes. You are about to meet the camp boss, Truck Eggers, and he looks much more formidable than Señor Foley. Also he seems to be very angry about something."

A man was approaching at a lumbering run. He apparently had been asleep in a hammock which Frank now discovered slung in the shade of smoke trees below the cutbank of the wash.

"It is best that I take care of this matter, amigo," Ramon said. "This one is dangerous. He has killed men, and some of them with his bare hands."

"Stay out of this," Frank said. "I tell you I don't want any gunshot wounds to take care of right now."

He had never before laid eyes on Truck Eggers, but he knew he was facing a different proposition than the flabby cook. He judged that Eggers must outweigh him by thirty, perhaps forty pounds, and all of it seemed to be brawn. The man had a shaggy mop of sorrel-colored hair, and his thick-boned face had not been shaved in days. He was bare to the waist, and his chest was matted with hair.

Truck Eggers was glaring, aghast, at the shambles Frank had created. He peered unbelievingly at Brick Foley. The cook, still dripping, was reeling groggily to his feet, but did not seem to know exactly where he was.

"What do you think yo're doin'?" Eggers screamed at Frank. He was apoplectic with rage.

"Looks like I've already done it," Frank said.

"Who in the flames air you?" Eggers frothed. He had slowed to a walk, but continued to advance, his fists knotted.

"I'm Frank Conroy, medical doctor for this division,"

Frank said. "I'm taking it for granted that your name is Eggers, and that you used to be camp boss here."

"I *am* camp boss here!" Eggers raged.

"Not any longer," Frank said. "You're fired, along with this lout of a cook here. You can deadhead back to Barstow and draw what pay is coming to you, but from then on you pay full fare. No more free rides. You've cost the company enough. A bunch of sick gophers could have turned out as much work as this camp has accomplished in the last month or so, according to the track boss at Barstow."

Eggers' florid face turned chalk-gray with greater fury. "Fired, am I?" he snarled. "By a liver-lilied dude like you? Not on your life. I'm camp boss here an' aim to stay boss."

Ramon spoke. "Dr. Conroy has the authority, Eggers. Pack your belongings and be ready to head out."

"Are you in on this, Zapata?" Eggers demanded. "If it's a gun fight you're tryin' to prod me in to, I don't fall fer it. I know you. I wouldn't stand much chance ag'in you. An' I'm not armed."

"That can be quickly corrected," Ramon said silkily. "Go get your gun. You are said to know very well how to use one. As for standing a chance against me that remains to be seen. I have been told you have killed men with guns as well as with your fists."

"No guns," Frank said. "Better get your gear and pull out when this string moves on west, Eggers. You're through here."

"But I'm not through with you," Eggers gritted. "I'll take care of you right now so that you'll never ag'in go around swingin' yore weight. But yore gun dog here will likely put a slug in my back. It wouldn't be the first time for him, if I size him up right."

"You are a liar," Ramon said softly. "Go get your gun. I will be waiting, and I will shoot you in the face."

"No," Frank said. "Back off, Ramon. This is my job. Stand over there with the crowd by the train so as to avoid temptation."

Ramon hesitated. "This one will be much tougher, amigo," he said. "He has gouged out the eyes of men. He will kick and bite and use the knee."

"So will I if he wants it that way," Frank said. "Take care of my shirt. I paid a dollar, two bits for it in San Berdoo. I only own one more, and good shirts are hard to come by out here."

Ramon reluctantly accepted the shirt Frank peeled off, and retreated across the spur track to stand among the spectators who were still staring.

Frank looked at Truck Eggers. "Let's get at it," he said.

Eggers measured Frank with eyes that were small and set deep between fleshy bones. He became suddenly wary as he saw that Frank was very broad of shoulder and equipped with long, lean-plated muscle.

Eggers decided on his plan of battle and came in crouching, swaying, arms hooked to clench in order to use the advantage of his greater weight. Frank did not wait to bear the brunt of that type of attack. He also moved in. Eggers had not expected that, and Frank's straight left jab drove him back on his heels and brought blood from a slashed eyebrow. He again attempted to close in, mauling with both fists and mumbling profanity.

The man was very strong and fairly fast on his feet for his size. One of his flailing fists penetrated Frank's defense and staggered him. Eggers rushed in eagerly to try to finish him. Frank crouched, dove forward, taking his opponent at the knees. He surged erect, sending Eggers in a crashing somersault over his shoulder. Eggers landed on his back on the mess table. That saved him from a more violent fall. He bounced off the table and came to his feet. He was only slightly winded by the fall. But he quit cursing. He was realizing that he had waded in deeper than he had believed possible.

Frank would not let Eggers choose the style of fighting. He was upon the bigger man, his left darting in and damanging an eye, his right exploding in Eggers' stomach. Eggers took that with a gasp of pain, waggling his head to clear his vision from the blood that was flowing from his gashed brow. Frank traded savage punches with him in a wild flurry.

Frank became aware of the acrid taste of blood—his own. Eggers again tried to clench, but Frank avoided that, knowing he likely could not survive infighting with the heavier man. He saw the hooked thumb of Eggers, groping to gouge an eye. He seized the thumb in his teeth and clamped down. Eggers uttered a grunt of agony. The man brought up a knee, trying to maim, but Frank had anticipated that, and it was his own knee that did damage.

That finished Eggers. The power went out of him. Frank broke free, smashed a left to the stomach and a right to the heart. He reeled back, watching Eggers pitch to the earth, writhing in a bloody daze.

CHAPTER 2

Frank inspected his hands, first of all, with the concern of a surgeon for his most valuable tools. He tested fingers and knuckles, and decided that while he could expect some swelling, no material damage had been done.

Ramon arrived at a run, seized his arm, and led him to the tank car where he began drawing water through the hose.

"Do not ever get angry with me, amigo," Ramon said. "It is not every day I have watched one man demolish two men so neatly. Stand there while I sluice the gore off you and find out where it is all coming from."

He washed Frank's face and upper body with water from the hose. The treatment revived Frank.

"You have an eye that may go into mourning, and you will talk with fat lips for a while," Ramon said. "All in all, you are in much better shape than I anticipated. It is the cut on the chin from which you bleed like the gored ox, but it is not deep, and a court plaster might do."

With Frank giving instructions, Ramon opened the medical kit, treated the wound with an antiseptic, and applied court plaster. He discovered that another person had approached and was watching the operation. The arrival was the tall Chinese who seemed to be the leader of the new crew of coolies, William Ling.

"Can I help?" William Ling asked.

"Ramon seems to have glued me back together fairly well," Frank said. "Thanks anyway, William Ling."

"And thank you for remembering my name," William Ling said. "And for the additions to our menu. They will be most welcome. Even we Chinese tire of rice and salt pork. But, above all, thanks for handling both of those rascals, particularly the big man. You have saved us much trouble."

Frank looked around. Truck Eggers was nowhere in sight. Nor was Brick Foley. Eggers evidently had recovered and had scuttled away, along with the cook.

William Ling was extending a hand. Frank tried to grin, but found the effort painful on his swollen lips. "Excuse me if I don't shake," he said. "My paws are hurting a little. But I don't understand. What do you mean by saving you from trouble?"

"Some of us, including myself, worked at a construction camp where Eggers was boss a year or so ago," William Ling explained. "He treated us as though we were even worse than beasts of burden. We did not look forward with any pleasure to being sent here to Pima Flat, knowing he was camp boss. But we could not refuse. Work is not plentiful for me and my companions."

"A new camp boss and a cook will be sent out as soon as I can get to Barstow," Frank said. "Ramon, here, will take over until the new man comes in. I believe you'll find conditions better here from now on."

Frank saw that Henry Sloan and his daughter were still standing alongside the sidetracked express, watching. Henry Sloan had his thumbs hooked in his belt, and his expression was that of disdain and disapproval.

"Where did you learn to box?" William Ling was asking.

"I went in for it to some extent in medical school," Frank

explained. "After I got licked a few times I found out that you have to get there firstest with the mostest, as one of the Civil War generals once said. I had a postgraduate course in the Army and in railroad camps."

"In addition to that, you are a doctah," William Ling said. "I envy you. It was my hope that I could become one of your profession. But it has not turned out that way."

"Look out!" Ramon shouted. At the same time he dove at Frank, taking him at the knees and pitching sprawling headlong into the shelter of the tank car.

The heavy roar of a shotgun blast was in Frank's ears. The gun had been fired near at hand. He also heard the sickening sound of a slug tearing into flesh and bone. The gun roared again.

Heavy pellets struck metal of the tank car above him. It was a buckshot gun that was being used, by the sound, and double-barreled. Both rounds had been meant for him, but Ramon's action had saved him.

He and Ramon rose to their knees, peering. Ramon's pearl-handled six-shooter was in his hand. Truck Eggers was the man who had emptied the two buckshot shells. He had armed himself to avenge the defeat he had suffered at Frank's hands.

Eggers stood there now, the gun smoke rising above him. He began making a frenzied attempt to reload the weapon but the fear of death was upon him now, for Ramon Zapata had lifted his six-shooter. Eggers would have died in the next instant, but Frank pushed Ramon's gun down and said, "No! No use killing him! Drop that gun, Eggers! Drop it, I say!"

Eggers, realizing he was being given a new lease on life, let the shotgun dribble from his hands. He stood waiting as Ramon walked toward him. He seemed to be staring wildly at something beyond Frank.

Frank heard a sighing sound and turned. "Great God!" he exclaimed.

William Ling had sunk to hands and knees, his head sagging. Blood was staining the hot soil beneath him. Frank leaped to his side and eased him to the ground. The blood was staining William Ling's cotton blouse. It was a chest wound. A heavy buckshot slug, or perhaps more than one, had struck the young Chinese.

Frank could hear the onlookers at the train still scattering for cover in case more shooting broke out. He ripped away William Ling's blouse. In that first glance he decided that only one wound was involved. The slug had entered William Ling's chest dangerously near the heart, but apparently had struck at such an angle that it had been deflected by bones and had followed a rib. It had inflicted a long ugly gash, and there might be bone damage. William Ling had escaped a direct heart wound, but loss of blood would nevertheless cost him his life within minutes without swift repair.

"My medical kit!" Frank barked at Ramon. "And my war bag. I'm short of bandages, but there's a spare clean shirt in the bag."

Sandals pounded the ground as William Ling's companions came at a run and surrounded them. Ramon handed him the medical kid and war bag, and Frank began working frenziedly. He located the slug just beneath the skin and extracted it easily, using a probe. Checking the loss of blood was another matter. He used sutures and clamps. He found the slim, ivory-colored hands of one of the Chinese helping him. Another of the watching Chinese slumped to the ground, his skin wan.

"Throw water on him and take him away," Frank said. "And if any more of you are going to faint at the sight of a little blood, do it somewhere else. I'm busy."

"William! William! Can you speak to me?"

It was the voice of the slim young Chinese who had been kneeling at Frank's side, helping him.

Astounded, he realized that she was feminine. Slim, young, but a woman. Like the men, she wore the same loose smock and pantaloons, sandals, and cone-crowned straw hat.

"Take this child away!" Frank snapped at Ramon.

"No! No!" the Chinese girl protested. "I am not a child. I will not faint. He is my brothah. My only brothah. Do not let him die, Doctah. Oh, see how he bleeds!"

Ramon tried to lift her to her feet, but she thrust his hands away. "I will stay," she said. "I will help."

"All right," Frank said. "Stay, then."

He was winning the battle to check the loss of blood. The Chinese girl helped as best she could, following his instructions. Her quick, sure fingers were needed. His fight with Truck Eggers had taken its toll. His hands were swollen, the fingers had lost some of their dexterity. The strain of the fist battle had snapped his stamina.

"We've got it," he breathed, looking for the first time at the Chinese girl, really seeing her. She was small, delicate of features, with intelligent eyes in the finely modeled face.

Frank became aware that a woman was screaming wildly. The sound came from the sidetracked train. The attention of the onlookers, which had been centered on Frank and his attempt to save the injured coolie, now swung to the vestibule of the forward Pullman.

"Dios mío!" Ramon exclaimed. "It is the señorita! Something has happened to her!"

Henry Sloan's daughter lay crumpled on the steps leading to the Pullman vestibule. Her aunt stood above her, and it was her voice that was sending out the eerie screaming.

In the excitement of William Ling's injury Henry Sloan's daughter had evidently lain unnoticed for several minutes.

Henry Sloan went stumbling to the steps of the car. "She's been hit!" he said, and his voice carried terrible grief. "My God! My daughter! She's dead!"

He lifted the limp form of his daughter in his arms. Frank saw the stain of blood. The father began to weep. "My poor, poor little girl!" he choked. His voice was wild and almost hysterical. "You must not die, Ellen, my darling! Not you too! Your mother is gone, your brother is gone. You can't leave me alone! You must not leave me!"

Then he added, a sudden frenzied hope in his voice, "She's breathing! You are alive, my darling! You won't die!"

His gaze fixed on Frank, who still knelt over William Ling. "You're a doctor," he panted. "Come here! What are you waiting for? Help my daughter! She's been hurt!"

Frank, still not entirely sure of success, continued final touches on the task of saving William Ling's life, working with renewed speed.

Henry Sloan placed his daughter's limp body in the arms of a frightened Pullman porter. "Take her to our compartment," he panted.

He left the car and came at a frenzied run across the spur track and seized Frank's shoulders, trying to lift him to his feet. "Are deaf?" he wheezed wildly. "My daughter needs you! My God, man, what's wrong with you? She might die!"

Ramon intervened, trying to force Henry Sloan away, but the gray-templed man, with a surge of frenzied strength, continued to try to drag Frank from his task.

"Blast you!" Sloan panted. "Can't you hear what I say?"

"I'll be with you in a second or two," Frank said, working with a final bandage. "I must finish what I'm doing. This man has lost too much blood."

"That chink?" Henry Sloan gritted. "You mean you're putting his life ahead of my daughter's? Oh no, you won't. You do what I say or I'll blow your head off. Damn you! Damn all doctors! One of your kind cost the life of my wife and my son. I won't let it happen again! My daughter is alive, but needs help! Listen to me if you want to stay alive!"

Frank found the muzzle of a weapon jammed against his temple. He looked up into the frenzied eyes of the man. Henry Sloan was plainly in a mental state to do just what he had threatened.

Again Ramon moved in. He seized Sloan's arm and wrested the weapon from his grasp. It was a derringer. "No! No, señor!" Ramon remonstrated, forcibly dragging Sloan back. "Get a grip on yourself. The doctor is doing all he can."

Frank finished his task. It was all he could do at the moment for William Ling. He leaped to his feet, seizing up his medical kit.

"Have your brother placed in the baggage car," he told the Chinese girl. "He's got to be taken to a hospital in San Bernardino. He must be kept quiet. I'll take another look at him as soon as possible."

Without a glance at Henry Sloan he headed at a run for the Pullman car and mounted the steps two at a time. The frightened porter and three or four other inquisitive passengers were crowded around the open door of a compartment down the narrow aisle.

He pushed them aside. Ellen Sloan had been placed on the lounge, for the berths had not been made up. Her aunt was bending over her, weeping and trying with shaking hands to dab with a lace kerchief at a crimson injury just above the girl's right temple.

Ellen Sloan's skin was waxen. She was breathing—irregularly, but breathing. There was no sign of any other injury. The shotgun slug had apparently grazed her temple. Evidently, having been at a greater distance than had been William Ling, the slug had been nearly spent when it struck her, for the wound was not too deep. However, the impact had been enough to stun her, at least. Her pulse was fairly encouraging, but her respiration remained irregular. It appeared to be more of a burn than a bullet wound, a type of injury with which Frank had become all too familiar in the Philippines. There had been little bleeding, for the slug seemed to have cauterized the skin. He held a vial of ammonia near the nostrils of the patient. That won results. Ellen Sloan's eyelids fluttered. She moaned and mumbled unintelligibly. Her hands stirred.

Her father had followed Frank into the compartment. "Thank God!" he hushed. "She's coming to. She's going to be all right, isn't she? Isn't she?"

The question was not a question but more of a peremptory command, an order. There was no sign of the derringer and Frank surmised that Ramon had taken it away from its owner.

But Henry Sloan's optimism and his demand were premature. Ellen Sloan sank back into that waxen-skinned inertia. Frank tried the ammonia once more. It had some result, but again she faded back into a coma.

He examined the injury through a surgical lens. It told him nothing. The slug seemed to have grazed the bone, but he had seen wounds almost similar that had amounted to little.

Henry Sloan uttered a moan. "Do something, man!" he

rasped. "She doesn't seem to be hurt bad. Why, that's hardly a scratch!"

Frank called for damp cloths or towels which the aunt flutteringly brought. He enclosed the girl's head in the cooling cloths. That produced results. Ellen stirred again, her movements stronger. She began mumbling again.

"It's concussion," Frank said. "All the symptoms. Like a punch to the jaw, except that she got it on the temple."

"You mean she'll be all right?" Henry Sloan demanded.

"That remains to be seen," Frank said.

"You mean . . . ?" The frenzy was returning to Henry Sloan's eyes, replacing the hope that had flamed there. He spoke again, his voice low, dangerous. "If my daughter, an innocent bystander, has to suffer because of some feud between you ruffians . . ."

He did not finish it. Frank ignored him and spoke to the flustered aunt. "Keep the damp, cold cloths on her. Get some ice and cool the bandages. That is the best thing for her in this heat. Keep her head cool."

He straightened, picking up his medical case. Henry Sloan blocked his path. "Where are you going?" the man demanded.

"I've got another patient to look at," Frank said.

"You mean that chink?" Sloan exploded. "You'd leave my daughter at a time like this to look after a coolie?"

"There's nothing more I can do here at the moment," Frank said. "I'm hoping your daughter will revive soon and that it is nothing more than having been stunned temporarily. I'll be back, of course, as soon as possible."

Sloan placed himself across the doorway. "Oh no, you're not!" the man said. "You're staying here until we're all sure my daughter is all right."

Again the derringer. Ramon had not disarmed Henry

Sloan after all. It was a double-barreled weapon, very deadly at such point-blank range.

Frank looked at the small gun. "I'm sure that even you would be hung if you pulled that trigger, Sloan," he said. "I'm beginning to believe that you need help as well as your daughter. Now, stand aside. I'm leaving."

He believed Henry Sloan was about to fire. Then a voice intervened. "What has happened? Where am I? Aunt Harriet? Dad? Are you there?"

Ellen Sloan was speaking. Her voice was thin and uncertain. The damp towel circled her head, covering her eyes. She instinctively started to remove it but found the effort too great.

"We're here, dear!" her aunt sobbed. "We're in the compartment. Thank God you're all right. You had an—an accident. But you're all right now."

Henry Sloan lowered the derringer. He shouldered past Frank and knelt beside his daughter. "You've been hurt, darling," he said. "It wasn't your fault. It was the fault of these railroad riffraff. They were fighting. You were grazed by a small pellet from a scoundrel's gun when he fired at another man, not caring that innocent persons like you were in the way."

Frank drew the aunt gently out of the way and lifted the damp cloth from Ellen Sloan's eyes. Her eyes were open, but they were still blank and confused.

"You seem to be all right, Miss Sloan," he said. He replaced the compress. "Keep the cold cloth on her," he instructed the aunt. "That seems to be the remedy. That and quiet and rest. I'll come back shortly and take another look at her if you wish."

"Don't bother," her father snapped harshly. "You're not needed. Don't forget that I'm holding you to account for the fact that my daughter nearly lost her life because of you. In addition to that you didn't seem to give a damn whether you gave her any help or not. I'll see to it that you are no longer working for this railroad as soon as I get to San Bernardino."

Frank looked at him. "Don't ever point a gun at me again," he said. "Don't ever."

"Dad!" Ellen Sloan exclaimed, her voice stronger, and startled. "Who's that? What does he mean about pointing a gun at him?"

Her aunt spoke soothingly. "Never mind, dear. It was nothing. Nothing at all. It's all over now. Just relax and don't concern yourself. Leave the cloth on your forehead. It seems to be doing you a world of good."

Frank left the compartment. Ellen Sloan was still weakly asking questions, insisting that someone explain what had happened. Her aunt was trying to smooth over her fears.

From the vestibule Frank could see that his order to place William Ling in the baggage car evidently had been carried out, for the area around the tank car and cooking area where he and Eggers had fought was deserted.

A locomotive whistle was sounding in the distance. The whistle on the sidetracked train answered, startlingly loud so near at hand as the engineer responded in railroad language, notifying the oncoming eastbound train that the main line was clear.

The disembarked passengers were piling aboard the cars, shoes clumping on steps and the wooden floors of the day coaches, seats creaking as they found their ways to their places.

Frank pushed among them, heading through the two day coaches toward the baggage car. The passengers were the customary assortment. They included Mormon families with numerous children, either bound for the new promised land in California or returning from a pilgrimage to view the temple and tabernacle in the mother home at Salt Lake City. Weathered desert men in worn boots, beards, and worn duffle bags on the racks were among the fares, along with three or four who by their dress were drummers for farm tools and hardware in their soiled white shirts, collarless, with neckties pocketed and boater straw hats in the racks. A bulbous-nosed drifter, probably ousted by the marshal from some settlement along the way, was already settling down to snore the hours away until he reached a new destination he knew not where or cared. Two nuns sat together in an end seat.

Frank noticed that the half dozen or so of the armed, hard-eyed men who had attracted his attention at Pima Flat seemed to have drawn together as a unit. They were pushing their way aggressively into the day coach through which he was trying to make his way. A plump traveling salesman who had settled down in a forward seat was forcibly removed from his position by a big, rough-voiced member of the group and told to find a location elsewhere. Which he did after a look at the odds against him.

Frank worked his way, along with the human tide, into the forward coach and finally was admitted to the baggage car by the baggageman. An army cot had been found on which William Ling lay. His sister was at his side, and she was overjoyed to see Frank.

"My brothah is still unconscious," she breathed. "I am afraid."

Frank used his stethoscope and pressure gauge. He nodded, satisfied, and smiled encouragingly at the Chinese girl, who had been anxiously watching his face, trying to read his thoughts as he worked. "Your brother is doing much better than I even hoped," he said. "You can quit worrying."

"You mean he will—will live?" she breathed happily.

"Unless he gets in the way of someone's buckshot gun again," Frank said. "He's got the constitution of a horse. He's not entirely out of the woods, of course. He lost a lot of gore, and he's still in shock, but coming out of it. He's young and strong and that's what counts. However, he'll have to take it mighty easy for a few days until he replaces that lost blood. I'll send word along to Joel Russell in Berdoo as to how to handle him. Joel is a doctor there and a friend of mine."

"Thank you, thank you," the Chinese girl breathed. "My brothah will always be grateful. I, too, will be grateful for what you've done."

"It's my job," Frank said. "What's your name?"

"I am Lily Ling," she said. "I was born in San Francisco, as was my brothah. I work for the railroad. I was to cook for my people at this camp."

She looked fondly down at her brother, smoothing back his black hair. "We have friends in San Bernardino who will help me look after him," she said.

"Fine," Frank said. "I'll ride along as far as Barstow, at least, and maybe on to Berdoo if it seems necessary."

"You put us far into your debt, Doctah," she said.

CHAPTER 3

The whistle of the eastbound express wailed near at hand. Sam Dobbs's voice sounded alongside the cars. "All aboard! All aboard! Step lively! All aboard!"

The last few passengers who had lingered, putting off until the last moment the ordeal of submitting themselves to the stuffy interior of the cars, came scrambling aboard. The engineer tooted the whistle as a reminder. The safety valve opened with a deafening rush of steam.

Sam Dobbs mounted the steps of the forward day coach and came into the baggage car. "How's the chink?" he asked, peering at the injured William Ling.

It was Lily Ling who answered, her voice crisp, resentful. "The doctah says the chink will live."

Dobbs did some sniffing from his bulbous nose at being put down by an Oriental, and a girl at that. He addressed himself strictly to Frank. "The young Sloan gal is settin' up already," he said. "They say it wasn't much more'n a scratch, but if I was you, Doc, I'd keep out o' Henry's way. He says it's a miracle his daughter's alive, an' no thanks to you fer not takin' the responsibility of attendin' her."

"Let him think what he wishes," Frank said.

"How about this one?" Dobbs asked, jerking a thumb toward the wounded William Ling.

"He's to be taken into Berdoo and to the hospital," Frank said. "He needs looking after. I'll deadhead as far as Barstow, and maybe all the way into Berdoo."

"What?" Dobbs snorted. "I don't see no cause to clutter up my baggage car with a yaller—"

"You see it now," Frank said. "He's an employee of this railroad, just like you and me, and is entitled to medical care when he's injured."

"It's yore funeral," Dobbs snorted. "I wash my hands of it."

Ramon Zapata had followed Dobbs aboard and was standing in the baggage car, listening. He had brought Frank's war bag. Sam Dobbs decided that his authority was being questioned and that his dignity was in danger. He started to swell up and bluster, but Ramon spoke in his mild voice. "It is best to do what the doctor says, Sam. He is difficult to get along with when he is vexed. Did you not see what happened to Eggers and the cook so recently?"

Dobbs was deflated and went away, blustering. Frank heard him, leaning from the steps of the day coach, shouting unnecessary orders to his flagman and the engine crew.

"And what about Truck Eggers?" Frank asked.

"I have placed him under arrest," Ramon said. "Did he not attempt to murder you? And did he not wound two other persons?"

"You're not an officer," Frank said, grinning.

"I am a special officer for the railroad," Ramon said. "At least Eggers thinks so. I'll turn him over to the sheriff sooner or later. Meanwhile I will keep him here at Pima Flat until a new camp boss arrives."

"What about Brick Foley?"

"Oh, that one. I will boot him aboard the first freight train that comes by. I do not believe you will have to give him any more baths in his own kettle."

"Thanks," Frank said.

"For what, señor?"

"For sort of letting Truck Eggers, and Foley also, know

that it might not be worthwhile to take another shot at me," Frank said. "Eggers especially. He's the kind that would carry a grudge. It's my hunch that he knows he might run into some bad luck if anything happened to me and you found out about it. In other words you put the fear of God in him."

"You rate me too high," Ramon said. "Perhaps it is the devil he fears. But I am sure you need not worry about him in the future. But . . ." Ramon hesitated.

"But what?

"Are you certain that the Señorita Sloan's injury does not amount to much?" Ramon asked.

"Apparently," Frank said. "Dobbs just told me that she is sitting up already. She seems to have been mighty lucky."

"I am glad," Ramon said. "It is my relief that both of you are lucky, you and the señorita."

"I see what you're getting at in your roundabout way of telling me something," Frank said. "You think Henry Sloan actually would have gone through with shooting me if his daughter had happened to have died from that buckshot slug."

"He had the look," Ramon said grimly. "I have seen it in the faces of other men when they were about to kill. He was loco at that moment. Some men get that way when they fear for those they love. And it is evident that he loves the señorita very much. I am happy that he did not go through with it."

"Why not?" Frank asked slowly. But he already knew the answer.

"He would be dead," Ramon said evenly.

Frank eyed him. "You really mean that, don't you?"

"I was told by Jim Beatty, my superior at San Bernardino, to see to it that no harm came to you," Ramon said, and his voice seemed casual. "He was thinking of this

Truck Eggers, of course, but he also said that good doctors are hard to find, and that the poor ones come by the dozen like eggs. He did not limit me to seeing to it that only Truck Eggers did not harm you."

Frank drew a long, deep breath. "Whew!" he said. "Ramon, you know that Henry Sloan measures forty feet tall in these parts."

"It happens that I am also your friend, Doctor," Ramon said. "I have seen you save the lives of countrymen of mine. The kind they call peons. I watched you today as you fought to save the life of that yellow coolie. To me, your life is much more valuable than that of Henry Sloan or that of his daughter. Henry Sloan has lived only for himself and his narrow ambitions. I do not know what ambitions his daughter has, but they must be shallow."

Frank had not realized how deep and deadly had been the aftermath of the injury to Ellen Sloan. "Thank God, it didn't come to that," he said. "You knew what you were risking if you had been forced to go through with it, don't you, Ramon? Of course you do. Henry Sloan may be arrogant and self-centered, but he swings great power in these parts. He has friends, influential friends."

"But none more powerful than my friend—and yours," Ramon said. His white teeth showed in a smile. He touched the pearl-handled pistol at his side. "No power on earth can change its rulings. But it is time for me to go. I say again that we were all fortunate. You, the señorita, Señor Sloan, and myself. It is as they say—all's well that ends well."

He turned to leave. "If it is ended," he added.

The eastbound express came roaring past, its whistle wiping out all vocal sounds. It kicked up a comet trail of alkali dust which drifted over the sidetracked train and on into the maintenance camp. It rolled on eastward with a departing wail from the locomotive. The roar faded off into the desert.

Frank halted Ramon, put a hand around his shoulder. "Thanks, amigo," he said. "*Muchas gracias!* Take care of yourself. When will we meet again?"

"Very soon, I hope," Ramon said. "Adiós." He left the baggage car and dropped from the steps of the day car as the train jostled into motion, the engineer taking the slack out of the couplings. He stood there, waving, as Frank peered back.

The string of cars lurched onto the main line and began picking up momentum westward. Frank took another look at William Ling. He opened his medical kit and administered an opiate.

"He'll sleep now," he told Lily Ling. "We're due in San Bernardino about nine-thirty. I believe I'll stay on into Berdoo. I have a friend there I enjoy seeing."

"A lady friend, of course," Lily Ling said. "You must have many of them." She was using her cone-crowned hat to fan her brother.

"How did you know?" Frank said.

"We Orientals are supposed to have mystic powers in such matters," she said. She was happy now that she felt her brother would live, and in a mischievous mood.

"Maybe they're not ladies," Frank said. "But speaking of ladies, I must go back down the line and take another look at the Sloan girl."

"Good luck," Lily Ling said. "From what your Mexican friend said you will not be welcome."

"Keep fanning," Frank said. "You stir up quite a breeze, both with the hat and your tongue."

He left her smiling at him and made his way back through the swaying day coaches to the Pullman. The door of the compartment that Ellen Sloan evidently shared with her aunt still stood open and he tapped on the wall outside, before presenting himself at the opening. "I am Dr. Conroy," he said.

Henry Sloan's bulk instantly barred the doorway. "I believe I told you that you're not needed here, Doctor, if you really are a doctor, which I doubt," he said.

"Are you sure?" Frank said. "I mean about my not being needed here?"

"Go back to your yellow friends," Henry Sloan said. "You seem to think they're worth more than my daughter's life."

Looking beyond Henry Sloan, Frank could see that Ellen Sloan was sitting up. She still had the cold, dampened towels wrapped around her head, masking her eyes. "Please, Dad!" she spoke. "Don't do anything you'll regret."

"Maybe I better take a look at you," Frank said.

Her father glared at him. "What good would that do? If you weren't sure about her, why did you leave in the first place? I'll have her examined by a competent physician when we reach San Bernardino. Good-by, sir."

Frank shrugged and left the Pullman. He returned to the baggage car. William Ling was sleeping under the influence of the opiate. He lingered for a time to make sure the patient was responding. "It's a case of letting nature take over now," he told the Chinese girl. "I'm going back into the coaches and stretch out. I'm about bushed. You should do the same. Your brother will sleep for the rest of the trip."

He left the baggage car. The forward coach was surprisingly filled, with no vacant seats, and he moved on to try the second car. He paused between the two coaches, grasping a handrail and balancing himself on the worn platform, letting the roar of the wheels, the rattle and rumble of couplings, and the rush of the wind enclose him. He removed his hat so that the wind could really touch him. It was a hot wind, a dry, arid wind, rough and challenging, but it was a cleansing wind, a wind that was laden with the wildness and freedom of this desert. He drew its promise deep into his lungs.

The day was dying. The sun was gone, and the fantastic twilight of the Mojave was painting hues of purple and ocher on the land—violent hues in a harsh world. To the north, the rims of the ridges and the crests of the great dunes of the Devil's Playground still caught the last rays of the sun, etching out weird shadows and monstrous shapes. The mind could imagine great beasts emerging from the caverns there, and believe stories of grinning skeletons—and of demons. At this time of day it was easy to believe all the legends surrounding the Playground.

It had been in Frank's plans to some day explore that awesome area. It was said to be the purgatory of lost souls, but, on the other hand, an old Piute chief for whom he had done a favor had told him that it was also a land of exquisite beauty. It was reputed to be totally arid, but there were also legends that there were springs and oases that some Indians knew about. If so, the tribesmen kept that knowledge secret.

These stories appealed to Frank's imagination and he hoped to attempt to determine if they were true. But he longed to explore the Playground principally because he wanted to gaze upon scenes no other white man had ever looked at—or at least had lived to describe. There was danger, of course. Many men had gone into the Playground and had never returned. Desert men claimed that their ghosts still guarded their graves in the fastnesses of the great dunes and blind canyons.

Frank catalogued many of the stories along with the

myriad of legends of the desert—tales of ledges of gold guarded by demented witch-hags, of silver hordes found in the labyrinth by men who had died of thirst on their way back, of Lost Dutchman and Lost Gunsight mines, whose locations had eluded their original discoverers. Some of these stories probably had bases of fact, no doubt, for the Playground, with its challenge of life or death, was a fertile breeding ground not only for fantasies but for the hopes of men to find wealth. Frank, in actuality, believed in none of the legends, but, for the sake of his unfulfilled dreams, he believed in all of them. To do otherwise was to deny himself the thrill of some day walking over new horizons, and even to gaze at the demons and the witch-hags.

The suppressed urges of his life were again taking him away from reality as he gazed at that distant, mysterious labyrinth past which the train was rumbling. For the moment he let himself be carried away from the bitter reality of the present, from the memory of the fight with Truck Eggers and its animal savagery, from the knowledge that with his bruises and hard-used garb he presented to people like Henry Sloan as wild an aspect as this land through which they were traveling. If there really were demons and witch-hags in that shattered land to the north, he wanted to face them, for he did not fear them. If there was beauty to be found, he wanted to revel in it. For he had his demons and witch-hags with him.

In spite of himself he returned to the stark bleakness of the present. Reality was the court plaster on his face, the ache in his hands and body, the heaviness in his swollen left eye. Reality was the memory of the blasts from Eggers' buckshot gun, and of William Ling slumping to the ground, of Ellen Sloan lying crumpled on the steps of the Pullman, of the frenzied glare in Henry Sloan's eyes above the pointed derringer.

He was suddenly limp of body and mind, almost exhausted. His thoughts went back over the events of his life, as one would finger the beads of a rosary—the privations he had endured to win his degree in medical school, the long months in Luzon. Before him once again were the pleading eyes of dying soldiers who expected him to save them, expected miracles. Malaria, bolo attacks by fanatical tribesmen, ambushes in the jungle, amputations, humid heat. Two years of it. Then return to civilization and its promises that had not been fulfilled. And now the desert. And the Devil's Playground.

He pushed open the door of the second day coach and entered. In contrast to the forward car there were many empty seats, and he saw the reason. The group of rough, armed men were occupying seats at the forward end of the car. They were noisy, quarrelsome, and drinking heavily. Four of them were engaged in a game of stud poker.

One, who was not in the game, was a paunchy, bull-necked man who, somehow, carried the air of leadership. Like the others, he had not shaved in days, but his beard was the heaviest, black, thick, and wiry.

Frank passed by the noisy group and took an empty seat as far as possible from them at the rear of the car. Only three or four other passengers were in the car, the remainder having preferred the more crowded conditions ahead.

Frank also began to regret his choice. He found himself facing the black-whiskered man who was occupying the forward seat which faced to the rear. He had the impression that he was being studied closely by the bearded man. He avoided that scrutiny, folded his lank legs into the space, and turned his attention to the darkening scenery through the window.

Two more passengers entered the coach, coming from the Pullman. One, to Frank's surprise, was Ellen Sloan. She was accompanied by her aunt. She still had damp cloths over her eyes and temple and was being guided by her aunt, who was fluttery and kept chattering instructions.

"There, there, dear!" the aunt said, finally steering the girl to a seat midway in the car. "You will only be here a short time."

Frank arose and moved to speak to them. "Are you sure your niece is up to this, ma'am?" he asked.

The aunt's nose tilted upward. "Oh, so it's you? I do not believe it is any of your concern, young man, but Ellen is all right. We came to this car while the porter is making up the berths, so that at least I can get a little rest before we reach San Bernardino. It has been a very trying day. Good evening, sir."

She spoke to the girl. "I'll be right back, dear. I want to make sure the porter follows instructions."

Frank waited until the aunt had left the car. "How do you feel?" he asked Ellen Sloan.

"I take it you are the man my father holds responsible for what happened," she said. "If so, please go away. Please."

Frank stood angry and helpless for a moment, then gave it up and returned to his seat. He was in no mood to humble his pride by pointing out how unreasonable she was.

Ellen Sloan huddled close to the car window. Despite the cloth over her eyes she kept her attention on the outer darkness. She kept fingering a small, gold locket that hung by a long, thin chain around her neck. Frank saw that her lips were moving. He realized that she was praying. Praying for what? It came to him suddenly that she seemed unutterably lonely and forlorn, as though she was entertaining the knowledge of a tragedy almost too great to bear.

He became aware of something else. Silence. The drunken, boisterous talk among the rough group in the car had ceased. The card game had ended. The half dozen men sat stiff and wooden, as though awaiting some signal.

Sam Dobbs came into the coach and moved down the aisle, pretending to examine the hat stubs of the few passengers, although he passed up the group at the front of the car.

He paused beside Frank's seat and bent close. "I don't like this," he whispered. "I smell trouble." His round face bore the sick sheen of cold sweat.

"What do you mean?" Frank asked.

"It's that bunch of hombres in the front seats," Dobbs answered. "They all got on at a flag stop about a dozen miles east of Pima Flat. They was scattered at first through both day coaches, but now they're bunched together. They're outlaws, or I never seen one. Ever hear o' the outfit thet calls theirselves the Jesse James gang?"

Frank had heard of such an organization many times. For the past two or three years the Southwest and particularly the desert area had been plagued by ruffians who had held up trains and mine offices and had raided small desert communities and ranches. They had terrrorized, murdered, and looted. The railroad, especially, had suffered heavy losses at the hands of the gang from raids on freight cars and mail cars as well as robbery of passengers. Even the army posts had been hit at times when the garrisons were weak.

The leader was said to profess to be the reincarnation of Jesse James, the outlaw who had been killed for bounty years in the past in Missouri. Imitating their leader, members of the outfit styled themselves under names equally as notorious. Sam Bass, Cole Younger, Bob Dalton, were some of the pseudonyms that had been adopted. They were all vicious killers, and the majority were known to the law by their real names.

"Do you think that's who they are?" Frank asked.

"I'm prayin' I'm wrong, but I got a gut feelin' thet I'm right," Dobbs breathed. "Thet big one with the crop of whiskers is the one what calls hisself Jesse James, or I don't know black from white. There's wanted posters out for him with a picture of him, but the picture was took when he was young an' smooth-shaved. He's wanted under his real name, which is Bart Haskell. I'm afeared it's him all right."

"What would they be up to?" Frank asked. "Is there anything up ahead that would be worthwhile?"

"Thet's just what's got me puzzled an' skeered," Dobbs husked. "Ain't nothin' worth mentionin' as fur as I know. If Wells Fargo was shippin' treasure, there'd be gun guards up in the baggage car, but there's only Charlie Frame, the mail clerk an' baggage smasher. He's pushin' seventy, an' likely ain't fired a gun in years. There's only four, five sacks o' mail, an' most of it looked like second-class to me when it come aboard at Salt Lake. Charlie said about all of it was Sears, Roebuck catalogues for people in San Berdoo. Speakin' of San Berdoo, I reckon you heard about the bank holdup there a few days ago?"

"I heard something about it," Frank said. "I was up in Nevada taking care of a track walker who had broken a leg. I didn't pay too much attention. There was some shooting, as I recall."

"Sure was," Dobbs said. "It was the James gang that was in on it. They run into some bad luck. The citizens came out smokin'. The gang didn't git a cent from the bank. They fought their way to the railroad roundhouse, stole a switch engine, an' got over Cajon Pass into the desert. They tore up some track in the pass an' cut the telegraph line an' got clean away before a posse could get goin'."

"Wasn't one of them caught?" Frank asked.

Dobbs cast an anxious glance toward the group in the

car. "Yeah," he whispered. "He's in jail in Berdoo, an' won't talk. The sheriff's purty sure thet a couple more of the gang was carryin' lead in their carcasses when they got away. There was dried blood in the cab o' the switch engine when it was found abandoned beyond Barstow. I'm tryin' to figure out what I ought to do."

"All you can do is wire ahead to the sheriff," Frank said. "And you might be barking up the wrong tree. Maybe they're only prospectors after all."

"I can't wire to nobody till we reach Barstow," Dobbs moaned. "At least without stirrin' up trouble. If it is them, an' I stopped the run at a way station, I'd likely git a bullet in my brisket."

Dobbs hurried away then, plainly not wanting to attract further attention from the rough-looking men. In fact Frank felt that such attention had already been aroused. He was sure the black-whiskered man was studying him with increasing speculation.

He settled back in his seat. He was unarmed. He owned a .44, but it was in his war bag, which he had left in the baggage car. Combating lawbreakers was not among his responsibilities. Except for forays, such as the one at Pima Flat where matters of health were involved, he let the appointed forces of law and order take care of the criminal element. In addition, he doubted that Dobbs's suspicions were justified. Dobbs had said there was nothing in the mail sacks that would be worth the attention of bandits. The pockets and luggage of the passengers in the day coaches might yield a few dollars and some cheap jewelry, but that would be about all, for there was little evidence of affluence among the coach travelers. The Pullmans might produce more pay dirt, with Henry Sloan probably the richest vein. Even so, there evidently were no more than a score of passengers in the Pullman, and several of them were children, from what Frank had seen. The profit there would be hardly worth the efforts of half a dozen or more men.

Lily Ling entered the coach. Her eyes sought out Frank and lighted. She shrank a little as she passed the silent armed men. One of them, Frank discovered, was an Oriental, like Lily, and he seemed suddenly greatly interested in the Chinese girl, his eyes following her as she hurried down the aisle.

She was aware of this, and it served to hurry her to seat herself beside Frank. "Ugh!" she breathed. "That man! Those awful men! They all need a bath if you ask me."

"How is your brother?" Frank asked.

"He is sleeping, as you said he would. I am sure he is much bettah, Doctah." She paused, gazing at him closely. "What is it?" she murmured. "You look strange."

"I'm not sure," Frank answered. "But whatever it is, here it comes."

A signal had been given and he was certain it had come from the big whiskered man. The armed group had suddenly leaped into action. They had come to their feet and had drawn neckerchiefs over the lower parts of their faces. They had guns in their hands.

Four of them rushed into the coach ahead. Frank heard two shots fired there. In the next instant two shots were fired deafeningly in his own car. They had come from the six-shooter in the hands of the big outlaw, and the bullets had been fired into the roof.

Ellen Sloan and Lily began screaming. Ellen Sloan started to rise, her head moving from side to side as though trying to find the source of the shooting. Lily Ling grasped Frank's arm with both hands. She was shaking with fright. "They're going to kill us," she moaned.

"Set still, yella gal!" the big man warned, grinning. "An' shut up. You too, white gal! An' all the rest o' you.

Nobody's been hurt—yet, but don't move unless I tell you to, or you'll shore wish you had minded me. I'm Jesse James, an' me an' my boys are takin' over this train for a little while. We'll be on our way after we git what we want. We ain't botherin' to rob you folks—this time. It don't look like it'd be worth our while."

Ellen Sloan started to remove the cloth from her eyes, then seemed to think better of it and let it remain. Lily Ling still clung tightly to Frank's arm. One of the outlaws who had remained in the coach was the Oriental. He was agate-eyed, pock-marked, with round brutal features, and evidently was a half-caste, the mixture of more than one race. He kept staring at Lily Ling with an expression that caused her fingers to tighten on Frank's arm.

Two of the outlaws hurried down the aisle to the rear platform. Frank heard the clank of metal as a coupling pin was pulled, then the pop of released compressed air. The speed of the train slowed, then quickened perceptibly. He realized that the Pullmans had been cut loose. At the same moment he heard gunfire from well ahead. He guessed the answer. Some of the outlaws had reached the engine cab by way of the baggage car and tender and had either shot the engineer and fireman or had them obeying orders.

"Just set tight!" the big outlaw repeated. He brought his gun to bear on Frank. "I'm talkin' to you 'specially, Doc. I seen you operate back there at the flat. You might be a dude, but you stacked up as hard formation to me. Don't git any ideas we'd both regret. We don't aim to do you any damage as long as you do as told. Whar's yore medical kit?"

"You seem to have the advantage of me," Frank said. "What did you say was the name?"

The outlaw scowled, then grinned. "Don't try to be cute,

Doc," he said. "I asked a question. Whar's yore medical stuff?"

"I left it in the baggage car," Frank said. "I have a patient there."

"Yeah, I know," the man said. "The chink what stopped a buckshot slug that was meant for you. Is he goin' to croak?"

"No," Frank said.

The man walked down the aisle and lifted the cloth from Ellen Sloan's eyes. Startled, she uttered a little cry of fright. "What about this one, Doc?" he said. "I heard say that she was lucky. Looks like I heard right. It ain't much more'n a scratch. I've been hurt worse by a deer fly."

He handed the damp cloth back to Ellen Sloan. He had to place it in her hands, for she seemed too stunned to move. "Take it easy, sister," he said. "Yo're goin' for a little ride with us."

"Ride?" Ellen Sloan echoed numbly. She hurriedly placed the damp cloth back over her eyes.

The man moved to a window and peered into the darkness. He seemed to be studying the outline of the ridges which were still visible against the sky. He suddenly nodded, reached up, and pulled the bell cord.

He spoke to Ellen Sloan again. "We're goin' hawsbackin'. There's no use tryin' to fight it. Ain't nobody who kin help you. I'm in charge. Me an' the boys."

"What are they going to do?" Lily Ling breathed.

Her words must have been inaudible to the outlaw, above the grinding of brakes and the squeal of wheels on the rails as the train suddenly began slowing, but he evidently had seen her lips move. "You there, slant-eyes! Keep your mouth shut afore I shut it for you with a chunk of hot lead. What are you doin' here with your betters anyway?"

The man was being dramatically tough and threatening —for effect, no doubt, in order to discourage anyone who might be thinking of interfering. However, Frank judged that he was the type who would shoot to kill merely for the sake of killing, especially when he had the upper hand.

"I'm Jesse James," the man repeated. "An' don't none of you forgit it. Clay, you git up to the baggage car an' see to it that the Doc's medical bag is brung along. All right, the rest o' you. Let's git ready to leave."

CHAPTER 4

The train was jolting to a stop. It had all taken place so swiftly that Frank had no idea of the elapsed time, but it could not have been more than a few minutes since Sam Dobbs had first voiced his suspicions of his group of passengers.

He was puzzled. Sam Dobbs had said there was no treasure aboard. Evidently he was right, for the outlaws did not seem interested in searching the mail car or the passengers. As for robbing the travelers in the Pullmans, they were now stranded on stalled cars down the track.

"Jesse James" still towered over Ellen Sloan. "Come on, sister," he said roughly. "As I said, yo're goin' for a little ride with us. Git on yore feet, sweetie."

Ellen Sloan did not respond. Her eyes masked by the cloth, her head was still moving from side to side as though she was trying by aid of hearing alone to fathom what was going on.

"Move!" the outlaw roared. "Are you deef?"

When she again failed to obey, he grasped an arm and dragged her roughly to her feet and pulled her into the aisle. "Do what I tell you!" he snarled.

She uttered a small, terrified scream. "Father! Aunt Harriet! Help me!"

"They ain't here," the outlaw snapped. "We turned their car loose. Now you listen to me an' do what I say."

"What do you want of me?" she choked.

"You'll find out," the outlaw said, and pushed her toward the door of the car. He again tried to snatch the cloth away from her head, but she grasped it, hanging on desperately, thwarting his attempt.

"Please!" she sobbed. "I need it."

"All right," the outlaw snarled. "But if yo're thinkin' of puttin' on a faintin' act fer sympathy, forgit it. I'll slap you red an' raw. Yo're Henry Sloan's daughter an' that means you've got snake blood in you jest like your paw. Yore kind don't cave in easy. So mind what I tell you or you'll wish you had."

Ellen Sloan did not faint. She did not attempt to scream. She was ashen, but her lips were set hard with contempt and fury, for the outlaw had again grasped an arm. She tore free with explosive strength. "You—you awful coward!" she panted.

She swung a palm with all her might. It caught "Jesse James" by surprise. It also caught him squarely on his whiskered cheek with an impact that sent him reeling.

He grasped the back of a seat for support and steadied. "Why, you hellcat!" he raged.

He ducked just in time, for Ellen Sloan was launching another blow. But she seemed off balance and it would have missed the target by a wide margin even if the outlaw had not taken evasive action.

She swung again with such force that she was whirled halfway around when she missed. The angry outlaw moved in, wrapped both arms around her, lifted her bodily. Kicking and trying to flail out with her arms, she was carried out of the car to the platform. She continued to fight fiercely, lashing out with both feet and trying to grasp her captor's bushy hair.

The big outlaw sat her on her feet and turned her over to two of his followers to be guarded. He backed into the coach, panting, hatless. Blood ran from fingernail gouges on his forehead. He glared balefully at his men, who still stood with guns leveled on the remaining occupants in the coach. They were obviously grinning back of their neckerchief masks, enjoying their leader's discomfiture. Under the blaze of his anger they tried to hide their amusement.

Frank realized that the big man was striding toward him. He found the muzzle of the six-shooter in the man's hand jammed against his chest. "All right!" the outlaw said. "Git on yore feet. Yo're goin' with us."

The ruffian silenced the question Frank began to frame. "Never mind askin' why. Jest do as I say if you want to stay alive. Git on yore feet, I tell you. You *are* a doctor. Don't bother to deny it. Yo're the railroad doctor an' yore name is Frank Conroy. We found that out from one o' the train crew at Pima Flat."

"Take this one too, boss," the half-caste said, pointing to Lily Ling. He whispered in the leader's ear, grinning.

The outlaw leader started to object at first, then grinned too and gave in. He reached past Frank, who had got to his feet and stepped into the aisle, and yanked off Lily Ling's straw hat, letting a plaited braid of dark, glossy hair fall below her shoulders.

"Danged if you ain't right," he said to the half-caste. "It is a she. A she-chink."

The half-caste dragged Lily Ling to her feet. She burst into a storm of terrorized weeping.

"Quit snivelin'," the leader snarled. "You ain't goin' to be hurt if you do as we tell you. We're all goin' for a nice, long ride in the moonlight. You, the doc here, an' the Sloan hellcat. We got use fer all three of you."

He prodded Frank with the muzzle of his gun. "Move!" he commanded. "Don't worry about your possible bag. We got plenty of anything you need in that line where we're goin'. Or else we kin git it in a hurry if need be."

Lily Ling clung to Frank's arm as he was marched to the platform of the car where Ellen Sloan was still being guarded. She had quit struggling and stood alone, her hair fallen, her cheeks stained with tears that had dried. Frank had the impression that, for her, tears were now a thing of the past, and she was accepting the inevitable.

One of the ruffians started to tear the gold locket from her throat, but the burly leader seized his arm, twisted it, and shoved his other hand into the man's face, pushing him back. "That's not for the likes of you," he snarled. "I might have use for that gadget, for the benefit o' all of us. Keep yore hands off it—an' off her!"

The ruffian stood there for an instant glaring at the leader, his jaw thrust out. Frank believed the man was about to make an issue of it. The leader realized this and backed off a swift pace, swinging his gun around to bear on his follower's stomach. "Go ahead," he growled tauntingly. "Go right ahead."

But the other man, with such odds against him, did not go through with it. "Take it easy, Bart," he said. "We're all in it together, ain't we?"

"Damn you!" the leader snarled. "What did I say about usin' real names? There's people listenin'."

"As if they didn't already know who you are," the other man responded. "Yo're famous, you know that."

Flattery succeeded. Bart Haskell, for there was no longer any doubt as to who the outlaw leader was in reality, let the matter drop. "Let's go!" he yelled. "Step lively!"

The outlaws leaped to the ground, and Ellen Sloan was handed into their arms. She once more fought valiantly, but futilely, for her strength was fading.

The half-caste descended and dragged Lilly Ling down

the steps to the ground. "You don't weigh more'n a bag of goose feathers, little gal," he said jovially. "Let's you an' me be friends, seein' as how we both got slant eyes. Some folks call me Hong Kong, but you kin call me dearie." He spoke the same rough, unschooled English of his companions.

"My brothah is in the baggage car," Lily Ling said pleadingly. "I must stay with him. He is wounded and may die."

"That's his bad luck," Bart Haskell said. "We seen what happened at Pima Flat, but he can't be too bad off if both you an' the doc here have left him alone. Anyway, yo're goin' with us, no matter what. We need the doc, an' we need a woman too, even if she is a chink."

He gave Lily a shove, and prodded Frank to follow in her footsteps. Blinded by the change from the lighted coach, he stumbled off the roadbed and found himself on loose desert soil. The outlaws were all piling off the coach and the engine.

One was brandishing a gold watch and chain. "Look what I got, Bart!" he exclaimed exultantly. "Tuk it off'n a drummer what don't need it like I do. I been wantin' a gold ticker fer a long time."

The outlaw leader cursed him savagely, seized the watch, and hurled it away into the darkness. "You lunkhead!" he raged. "Didn't I tell you not to bother the passengers? What if one of 'em had come up smokin' like them citizens did in Berdoo? I ought to put a slug in you. We might have got ourselves into another shoot-out. No tellin' how many of them passengers had hardware hid under their seats."

The crestfallen man slunk back among his companions. Lily Ling wrested herself from Hong Kong's grasp and scurried to Frank's side. She was trembling. Ellen Sloan stood straight and silent nearby. The outlaw leader grasped her arm, but she threw it off with a new, fierce surge of scorn.

"Still spunky, ain't you?" Bart Haskell gritted. "You'll learn better'n to treat me like dirt afore we're through with you, Miss High-an'-Mighty. Git movin'!"

He snatched the cloth from her head. "You don't need this no more," he said. He pushed her roughly ahead. She stumbled and fell. Frank moved in, intending to assist her to her feet, but she arose quickly, needing no help.

Haskell shouldered him back. "You toe the line, Doc," he said. "Do only what I tell you. I've killed my share of fools like you. Keep that in mind."

Frank was recalling what the wanted posters had said about this man who professed to be the reincarnation of Jesse James, but whose real name was Bart Haskell. He was wanted in many places for a series of crimes, ranging from petty robbery to murder. From back-alley sluggings in cattle and railroad towns he had graduated into a full-time career as the head of this band of cutthroats. He had served a five-year term in Yuma prison in the past, but that had apparently only whetted his appetite for preying on society. Haskell was in his mid-forties now, probably nearly fifty, and had the brains and dominating ability to maintain control over his wolf pack.

Haskell pushed Frank ahead so roughly he reeled against Ellen Sloan. She would have fallen again, but he grasped her in time and managed to steady her on her feet. Even so she seemed bewildered, staggering a trifle. He swung her around in the direction the outlaws wanted them to go and they stumbled along, side by side.

They had put some distance between themselves and the lights of the stalled train when Frank, his eyes now fully adjusted to the starlight, realized that horses were waiting ahead. There was a considerable number of animals, some saddled and some on picket. Along with them were four or five pack mules that were loaded with what were apparently sizable water bags. Two men, who seemed to have been in charge of the waiting remuda, came striding to meet Bart Haskell.

"How'd it go, boss?" one of them asked, peering at the captives. "Looks like you got more'n you bargained fer."

"How else would it go with me runnin' the show?" Haskell boasted. "We got what we went fer, an' a couple o' things more."

"You didn't seem to run things quite as slick at Berdoo a few days ago, Bart," one of the others observed. The speaker was the burly outlaw who had rubbed Haskell's fur the wrong way earlier.

Haskell whirled on him. "You keep gittin' smart with me, Pete," he said, "an' you're likely to run into some mighty tough luck. It wasn't my fault things went wrong there an' you know it, but if you want to make somethin' of it . . ."

Again the outlaw shrugged it off. The two men who had been waiting in charge of the horses were still peering in wonder at the captives. "Who's this here gal, boss?" one asked. "Wasn't you supposed to grab on to Henry Sloan? Anyway she's a looker. A real looker if'n you ask me. An' ain't this small one a chink? What do you want with a chink? Who's the tall hombre?"

"I'll write you a letter about it," Haskell sneered. "Right now, let's git movin'."

Haskell picked Ellen Sloan up in his arms. She cried out and began to struggle. "Quit it, you fool!" Haskell snarled. "I'm only settin' you on a hawss. You kin ride, I hope. If not yo're goin' to learn in a hurry."

Another of the outlaws was lifting Lily Ling onto a

horse. "Hey, boss!" he exclaimed. "This here chink is a gal. A chink gal, fer gosh sake."

"Shut up!" Haskell snapped. "O' course she's a gal. Thet's why we brung her along. Let's pull out. We got to be makin' tracks. The wind will be comin' up soon."

Frank was shoved toward a horse. "Git aboard that cayuse, mister," an outlaw said. "I seen you handle them softies back there at Pima Flat, but they was flabby an' couldn't take a punch. Me, I'm different. I'm Sam Bass. Ever hear of me?"

"Nothing good," Frank said.

The outlaw laughed, pleased. He was the one who had crossed verbal swords with Bart Haskell. He might claim to be known as Sam Bass, but Frank had heard Haskell address him by the name of Pete.

Pete barged belligerently against Frank. "Take a swing at me, fella," he said. "Go ahead."

"Some other time," Frank said.

He found the stirrup of the horse that was being held for him, and mounted. Bart Haskell handed him the medical case and he balanced it across the pommel. The horse was equipped with a Whitman army saddle, a type with which he was well acquainted. The animal kettled a little, but he quickly notified it that he was in charge.

He peered down at the outlaw who had hazed him. The man sized up as big, brawny, and arrogant. He was proud of his physical prowess and his toughness. He proved it in the next moment by shouldering roughly into one of his companions as they moved about, tightening cinches and coiling picket lines. He shoved the man out of his way.

"What'n hell, Mace!" the outlaw yelped. "Don't you never walk around nobody that gits in yore way?"

The burly outlaw gave the speaker a vicious shove that sent him somersaulting head over heels over a stunted bush. "My name's Sam Bass," he rumbled. "Remember to keep usin' it in front of strangers."

Frank had heard of the pseudo Sam Bass also. An outlaw, whose real name was Pete Mace, was listed on wanted posters as one who called himself Sam Bass. Mace had operated as a cheap pugilist in bare-knuckle ring contests until he could find no opponents who could match his butting, gouging, and mauling. Then he had turned to robbery.

Frank heard Lily Ling sobbing. He kneed his horse close to her side and laid a hand on her arm. "Steady," he said.

"What will they do with us?" she wept.

Ellen Sloan was nearby. She was trying to arrange her skirts as she sat astride the saddle onto which Bart Haskell had placed her.

"Are you all right, Miss Sloan?" Frank asked.

She did not answer, and he repeated the question. Then she spoke—without looking at him. "Are you the man who is responsible for all this?" she asked icily.

"But—!" Frank began.

She stirred her horse, moving it farther away. She did not speak again. There was no need. She had placed a wall between them. There was no forgiveness in her.

The outlaws were mounting, saddles creaking, horses grunting and rebelling. Bart Haskell brought his horse to Ellen Sloan's side and took the reins from her hands. "I'll lead you fer a while," he said. "Hang onto the horn if'n you can't stay tight in the saddle."

She continued to remain silent. She did not need to grasp the saddlehorn. Even without the reins in her hands Frank saw that she seemed to be at home on a horse.

The cavalcade set out, heading north, away from the railroad right of way through the thin, thorned desert growth. A glow to the east announced the coming of a moon that would be just past the full. White stretches of alkali served to break the darkness and aid the eyesight of horses and humans.

Lily Ling remained close at Frank's side. She had stopped sobbing, and although she was evidently not experienced in the saddle, she rode lithely, responding to the animal's erratic gait as it worked its way over the loose, uneven surface.

They were boxed in by outlaws. Frank counted noses and saw that there were nine men in the group. Bringing up the rear were loose remounts, hazed along by two more riders. The lights of the train faded and receded into faint dots as the cavalcade proceeded. Frank heard the thin, distant hiss of steam from the boxes, and the throb of the stack. The engine crew was getting the broken string into motion, returning, no doubt, to pick up the abandoned Pullmans. Finally Frank could make out the lights no more. There was only the desert stars, dimming now as the moon rose.

Ellen Sloan rode in silence. She sat straight on the horse, her back turned uncompromisingly on Frank. Suddenly Lily Ling spoke. "You are being foolish, Miss Sloan. The doctah is not to blame for all this. My brothah was shot also, but it was not the doctah's fault."

That penetrated the shell into which Ellen Sloan had drawn. She turned in the saddle. "Your brother? I did not know. Was—was he—he killed?"

"No," the Chinese girl answered. "He will live, thanks to the doctah. He was badly hurt. Much more so than you. I would say that if anyone is to blame for getting us into this awful thing, it is you, Miss Sloan."

Ellen Sloan did not debate that or respond. Presently she said, "I am glad for your brother. Glad he will live." There was a darkness in her, a bitterness that chilled Frank.

She turned away again, retreating into the shell of remoteness and hostility. They rode on, the outlaws letting the horses pick their own way over the yielding desert soil and among the tough clumps of cactus and boulders.

The moon labored its way into the sky. The light only served to bring out the lonely majesty of their surroundings —and its desolation. This land had suffered cruelly under the suns of the ages. The phalanx of tiny spines on the cholla cactus glistened as though frost-covered. Deerhorn clumps formed traps into which a man could fall and be tortured. Stands of ocotillo rose here and there, their whiplike fronds almost reptilian in the moonlight. Saltbush fringed the alkali flats, vying with creosote brush, whose small leaves reflected the moonlight as though greased. Burroweed tried to repel them from ascending the rises.

The dunes and ridges of the Devil's Playground took shape ahead, but seemed to come no nearer as the animals, now resigned to the task, plodded along. The outlaws, at first talkative and jubilant over the success of their mission, became more and more silent as though waiting in suspense for something. The hoofs of the horses were now swishing through loose sand that seemed to be ever deepening—the advance guard of the great dunes ahead.

Bart Haskell finally broke the silence. "Blast it, won't that wind ever come up? We'll be in a hell of a fix if it quits on this night of all nights!"

Frank twisted in the saddle and looked back. The tracks the many shod hoofs were making remained very distinct in the sand, leaving a trail that extended as far as vision could carry.

Haskell called a halt. He glared at the sky and lifted a clenched, threatening fist. "Blow, damn' you!" he raged. "Blow!"

The words faded off emptily into the desert. No echo

came back. Uneasiness deepened among the ruffians. They slid from the saddles, glaring at the sky, waiting. The captives remained mounted.

"What'll we do if'n the wind don't come up tonight, boss?" one of them croaked anxiously. "There'd be a posse on us before dark tomorrow. Jim Driscoll will be sendin' out horses an' men by special train by daybreak if'n he kin round 'em up in San Berdoo by that time. We ought to have cut that telegraph line."

Haskell cursed him. "You fool! We need that telegraph line ourselves. We need it bad. Keep yore shirts on, all of you. It's early yet. It never does start blowin' real good till well along toward midnight."

"They need the wind to cover their trail into the dunes," Frank murmured to Lily Ling. "On the desert it always springs up about this time of night and blows hard until toward daybreak. Then it stops and there's a dead calm. The Indians call it the Devil Wind around here. It has another name. The Arab camel drivers the army brought over after the Civil War to pack supplies across the desert called it the sirocco. Like on the Sahara it blows at night in summer here on the Mojave."

She peered toward the ghostly loom of the sterile dunes ahead. "They say there's no water in that awful place, no living thing but tarantulas and serpents," she said. "My brothah told me about it only today as our train passed by this terrible place on the way to Pima Flat. They say nobody has ever come out of it alive."

"It's rough and tough in there, no doubt," Frank said. "But it can't be quite as bad as all that. These outlaws seem to know something that nobody else knows. At least the Playground seems to be where we're heading."

One of the desperadoes moved in and lifted Ellen Sloan from her horse. He was the swaggering, aggressive Pete

Mace. Now that the neckerchief had been removed, his features were wolfish and savage. Ellen Sloan, startled, cried out angrily and tried to strike him.

Frank slid from his horse. He moved in, snatched off Mace's hat, and grasped a handful of hair. He yanked the man's head back so violently he feared for a moment he might have broken his neck. But the outlaw's only injury was to his pride. He released Ellen Sloan, screeched an oath, and came at Frank with fists poised. But Bart Haskell intervened, stepping between them and pushing Mace back.

Haskell was grinning. "Simmer down, Pete," he said. "You ought to know better'n to try to git cozy with our lady friend. If the doc here hadn't stepped in, I'd have had to chastise you myself."

"I kin lick you anytime, day or night, an' twice on Sunday," Pete Mace said. "You know thet, Bart."

"I wouldn't bother skinnin' my knuckles on you, Pete," Haskell said, and his grin had turned ugly and deadly. "I'd shoot you right through the guts. If you want to try it that way, go for yore gun."

Pete Mace evidently was out of his depth when it came to matching gun speed with the outlaw leader. "Aw, I didn't mean nothin', Bart," he growled, and turned away. "I jest figgered she might as well git off'n that horse fer a spell."

Haskell whirled, addressing all of his followers, and his voice was as ugly as had been his grin. "That goes for all of you," he said. "Hands off. Pin that in yore bonnets, an' keep it there. No rough stuff, at least till we git my son out of the hoosegow in Berdoo an' safe back with me. You hear me?"

There was a mutter of consent. None of them apparently had any desire to challenge Haskell's leadership. At least at the moment. Only Pete Mace spoke. He addressed Frank. "You'll regret that you laid a hand on me, you dude. Nobody kin maul me around when I wasn't ready an' not pay fer it."

CHAPTER 5

Along with the neckerchief masks, the outlaws had shed the bombastic pseudonyms and were now using their real names—or at least the names they were known by among their kind. Frank had also learned one more important item. Bart Haskell had a son, and that outlaw was the one who had been captured during the gang's attempt to rob the bank in San Bernardino a few days previously. Haskell's son was a prisoner in the San Bernardino jail.

He discovered that Ellen Sloan was on her knees, scrabbling around with her hands in the sand, searching for something. He saw that her gold locket was missing. It lay in plain sight on the ground, shining in the moonlight, but she did not seem to notice it. She had lost it during the struggle with Mace.

He moved in, picked up the ornament, and offered it to her. "Here it is," he said. "The chain was broken."

She seemed dazed, for she groped for the locket, but kept missing until he pushed it directly into her hands. She ran her fingers over the chain and began managing to knot the slender links together.

"Thank you," she said rigidly. She turned her back on him, then stood there, alone, unapproachable.

Frank gazed at her. A dark presentiment had been growing within him that there was something very much out of the ordinary with Ellen Sloan. There was something wrong with her, either emotionally or perhaps mentally. This last possibility drove horror through him.

He now had the reason for her presence here as a prisoner. Ellen Sloan was a hostage to be held as human ransom for the release of Haskell's son from jail.

No doubt she was aware of this also, for she must have heard, as he had, the mention that Haskell's son was a prisoner. Frank also believed he knew why he was being taken to the outlaw hangout. He remembered that two members of the gang were believed to have been wounded in the gun fight at the bank in San Bernardino. If there were wounded men in the outlaw hide-out, they probably were in need of medical help. Bart Haskell had taken advantage of the luck of finding a doctor aboard the train on which Ellen Sloan had turned out to be the real obective. That explained why he had made sure the medical case was brought along.

However, none of this explained why Lily Ling had also been made captive. The answer to that was hidden somewhere in the whispered request the half-caste had made to Bart Haskell in the railroad coach.

The outlaws were moving restlessly about, growing more and more nervous. Some were rolling cigarettes, others working on cuds of tobacco or chewing the stubs of cigars. Haskell chomped on an unlighted cigar and kept glaring at the sky as though to insist by unspoken threats that it do his bidding.

Pete Mace, taking advantage of the situation, pretended to barge into Frank by accident, nearly knocking him off his feet.

He steadied, and found himself eye to eye with his tormentor. "Want to make somethin' of it, Doc?" Mace jeered. "This is as good a place as any."

Haskell again intervened, shouldering between them. "I'm tellin' you fer the last time to take it easy, Pete," he growled. "There's a right time fer some things an' a wrong time, an' a lame-brain like you always wants to pick the wrong time. I've got plans fer the doc, here, an' until I say the word you keep away from him. You'll git yore chance, but it's me thet'll pick the time an' place. You hear me?"

"All right, all right," Mace said, grinning. "That's a promise I'll hold you to, Bart. All I want is the chance. I just want this dude to keep in mind what's comin' to him when you say the word. That is, if you ever git around to sayin' it."

"What do you mean, if I ever git around to it?" Haskell demanded dangerously.

"Maybe I ain't the only lame-brain in this outfit," Mace said. "There're some of us what ain't so sure where the brains air after that shoot-out in Berdoo. It ain't our fault Clem's in jail an Blackie an' Denny got hit. It looks like we're all riskin' bein' hung jest to git Clem out. Woman-stealin' is looked on mighty hard in these parts."

Pete Mace swaggered away and Haskell did not pursue the matter. Lily Ling had dismounted, and was at Frank's side. "He is a very bad one," she breathed, her voice shaking. "A beast. Some time or other he will try to fight you."

"Not if I can wriggle out of it," Frank said. "He would be very hard to handle. Likely he's only trying to throw a scare into me."

"I am scared, even if you are not," she said. "That beast and the one who called himself Jesse James are not friends. The beast would like to take over leadership of these awful men. And you are, what you call it, caught in between."

"You might be right," Frank said.

"They are taking Miss Sloan because the son of the leader was captured in San Bernardino," she said. "And they are taking you because two of them are wounded. But why are they taking me?"

"Try not to let them know you are afraid," Frank said. "They're the kind that like to take advantage of weakness in others. Like rats. Like hyenas. Stand up to them."

"I am a woman," she said grimly. "Is that why I am here?"

"I believe there must be some other reason," Frank said.

"It is because of that ugly one, the one they call Hong Kong, that I was seized," she said. "He is only partly Chinese. And all of him is evil."

"Quit that palaverin', you two," Bart Haskell snapped. He caught the Chinese girl by the arm and forced her apart from Frank.

Silence came again. The wait went on, with the outlaws growing more and more nervous. Frank found a boulder on which to sit. He spoke to Ellen Sloan, who still stood rigid and silent, ignoring the movement around her. "There's plenty of room," he said. "We might be in for a long ride. Better take it easy."

She did not speak or make any sign that she had heard. Lily came to her side. "You really should try to relax, Miss Sloan," she said.

She responded to the Chinese girl. "Thank you," she said. She seemed uncertain as to direction and let Lily guide her the few steps to a boulder. The Chinese girl sat with her for companionship.

A sigh arose among the outlaws. Frank felt the first stir of a real breeze on his cheek. "Here it comes!" one of the outlaws breathed almost prayerfully. Then louder. *"Here it comes!* The wind! The Devil Wind!"

The sirocco arrived gently at first, then briskly. It grew in strength. The thorned growth began rustling a weird chorus. Sand began to blow. The outlaws whooped gleefully, their fears vanishing.

"Mount up!" Haskell shouted jubilantly. "Let's go!"

Ellen Sloan and Lily were lifted onto their horses. Frank was prodded into swinging aboard his mount. The wind steadily picked up power as they rode on through the moonlight, which turned from pale silver to an eerie, tarnished copper hue as sand and dust rose higher against the sky.

Looking back, Frank could see that the tracks the horses made in the loose going were sure to be wiped out within the hour.

Haskell was looking back also. He laughed with glee. "Henry Sloan an' Jim Driscoll kin send a hundred men out here tomorrow an' all they'll do is waste time an' sull horseflesh," he said. "Ain't a white man alive that knows the Playground like we do. Some o' them Piutes or Pimas kin track a flea across an eggshell, but they got no stomach fer goin' into the Playground. They think the devil lives there."

"And his name is Bart Haskell," Frank spoke. "Otherwise known as Jesse James."

Haskell whirled in the saddle, scowling. But that changed to an ugly grin. He suddenly had decided to be flattered. "Correct, Doc," he said. "An' keep that in mind."

They rode on. The wind droned around them. Sand blew stingingly and they drew up collars and bent hats against it to shield their eyes and faces. The horses, heads drooping, plodded disconsolately through the going that steadily grew heavier, for they were among the big dunes now. The moon swam higher in the metallic sky. After a time Haskell called a halt to freshen and water the horses. Water was passed around to the riders and captives in tin cups. Frank drank. The water had the brackish taste of metal and he guessed that it had come from a railroad tank car—perhaps stolen even from the one at Pima Flat or perhaps with the connivance of Truck Eggers. Fitting together the pieces of knowledge he had picked up about these men, it seemed that they must have emerged from their hide-out the previous night, made their way to the flag stop east of Pima Flat by some means or other, and boarded the westbound train on which the Sloans were traveling. That meant they had advance information that Ellen Sloan was on the train.

They mounted again and pushed ahead, slow mile after slow mile. From the position of the Big Dipper in the sky Frank estimated that the hour was well past midnight and they now seemed to be hopelessly circling in a maze of swales between dunes and jagged ridges whose crests often cut off the moonlight. He saw that Haskell was setting a westerly course almost at right angles to the northward route they had been following, and surmised this was a plan to make it more difficult for any searchers to estimate the exact direction the outlaws had taken into the Playground.

Haskell began pushing the weary horses. It was obviously now a race against the coming of daybreak, for Frank knew that the Devil Wind soon would die and the desert would lie still and motionless and even chilly, awaiting the warmth of the sun.

They emerged from the big dunes into a still more unreal world of sterile, volcanic ridges, rising from an undulating sea of white sand. They rode on into black draws where the only sound was the echoes from the shuffling of hoofs in the soft underfooting.

They emerged into moonlight once again and Haskell called a halt. Some saddles were shifted to fresher mounts from animals that were fading. Water was again apportioned. From the condition of the stock Frank decided that these animals had been used to make the long trip to the flag stop east of Pima Flat the previous night and day.

The weary ride was resumed. Lily Ling was drooping in the saddle. Frank rode close at her side, ready to seize her if she collapsed. But she straightened, gave him a little resigned smile, and said, "I am all right. I—I fell asleep. I was dreaming—dreaming that I was home in San Francisco, drinking tea with my mothah and fathah, eating rice cakes."

Haskell was close by, listening. He uttered a sardonic laugh. "You'll get no rice cakes where we're goin'," he said. "Neither will you, Doc. But we got plenty of most everything else, includin' booze. You name it, we got it—or we kin git it if we decide to try."

The wind faded to wispy gusts, then died. The sand around them was now thin and studded with shards of weathered rocks. The shattered ridges and a few dunes loomed on all sides, but the route Haskell followed carried them through swales and deep draws. The penetrating chill of the desert dawn moved upon them. Frank could hear Lily Ling's teeth chattering. The heat of the previous day was only a memory.

The night surrendered to the rose-tinted dawn. The desolation of the land came out of the shadows, emerging like a prehistoric monster from the deep. Stark ridges had scaly flanks and peaks like fangs.

They entered what seemed to be a narrow rift in a sheer wall. The rift was a mere slit in which they rode single file with the walls so close on either side they could be touched by outstretched hands. The slit continued on and on. The growing daybreak could be seen only in the thin channel of sky far above them.

However, the heads of the tired horses began to lift and their pace quickened a trifle without urging. Frank caught it also, the unmistakable fragrance of greenery and, above all, the life-sustaining promise of water.

They emerged abruptly from the slit into open daylight. Ahead lay a large flat, surrounded on all sides by ridges and the crowns of dunes. Frank saw the glint of open water, an oasis of astounding size. Gnarled mesquite and marsh grass grew in the boggy fringe of the pond, with clear water beyond. Half a dozen native palms flourished at the far end of the pond. Birds fluttered and chirped. Crickets were still sounding. Beyond the pond was a sizable flat where grass grew and a few horses and mules were grazing. Grain, in sacks, was stored back of a fence of smooth wire. A blacksmith forge and anvil stood under an awning made of dead palm fronds, with tools handy. The shop was deserted at this hour, the forge fire dead, but from the accumulation of grime it evidently had seen much service, proof of the length of time the oasis had been occupied.

The occupants themselves used the shelter of a camp of scattered tents and reed-built shacks. A cooking area that was almost a replica of the one at the Pima Flat railway camp flanked the nearer tents. It stood under an awning made of canvas. Beyond the huge cookstove stood a great collection of barrels and boxes of supplies.

Three men came from the tents, stuffing shirts into breeches, and arrived on the run, shouting greetings. A woman emerged from a tent that was set well apart from the others. She was a Chinese woman, big with child. She stood staring for a moment, then retreated back into the tent.

The outlaws dismounted and began flexing stiffened muscles and joints. "How're the boys?" Haskell asked the men who came running up. The arrivals were staring at the captives.

"Blackie ain't as bad off as Denny," one of them answered, still peering at Ellen Sloan and Lily and Frank. "At least he kin cuss, but we're shore worried about Denny. That laig looks mighty bad. Say, how many folks air you bringin' to camp, Bart? Ain't thet chink a she-gal? An—"

Haskell didn't bother to answer. He whirled on Frank. "You heard what he said, Doc. Yo're needed. That's why I brung you. Come on!"

He seized up Frank's medical kit, pulled Frank along with him, and headed toward one of the tents. Ellen Sloan had slid from the horse. She still had a hand on the saddle as though to balance herself. She happened to be directly in Bart Haskell's path. Frank expected her to move out of the outlaw's way, but she did not. She turned her head in his direction, and Haskell took that as an act of defiance. It was not. Frank realized the full truth at that instant. But not Haskell. He jammed violently into her, nearly upsetting her. She managed to avoid falling by grasping the stirrup. She pulled herself erect and seemed to be again defying Haskell.

Haskell slapped her, sending her reeling. "You'll learn to git out o' my way when I come along, Miss High-an'-Mighty," he snarled. "I'll teach you that, even though yo're Henry Sloan's whelp, you don't own the earth."

He would have struck her again, but Frank leaped forward and caught his arm in time to stay the blow. He grasped Ellen Sloan by the arm. She was reeling, but she steadied and clung instinctively to him for support. She was quivering violently. Her face was dead white, her lips ashen.

Her eyes were a deep violet shade beneath finely arched brows. Those violet eyes were turned on him at this close range as though in desperate search of something tangible to which to cling. Eyes that were beautiful and desperate—and utterly blank.

He turned and looked at Bart Haskell. "She's blind!" he said.

Haskell halted dead in his tracks, his head turtling higher

on his thick neck as he stared unbelievingly. "What'd you say?" he croaked.

Frank did not bother to answer. He spoke instead to Ellen Sloan. "It's true, isn't it?"

"Does it matter now?" she answered. Her voice was level, but very bitter, very resigned.

Frank moved close to peer at the dark, crimson line above her temple. More than before the injury seemed minor, little more than a deep scratch that apparently was already healing itself. But in him was a cold horror, a vast and cold protest. The dread intuition that had been building up within was grimly justified.

"How long have you known?" he asked hoarsely.

She shrugged. "That does not matter either."

Dead silence had fallen as the outlaws stared, still unable to believe what they were seeing and hearing. Frank placed a hand under Ellen Sloan's chin, lifted her head so that he could see the pupils of her eyes more clearly. They told him nothing.

"It's probably only temporary," he said, and found that his voice was shaking. "It's happened before. Pressure on the optic nerve, perhaps a form of trauma from the shock of the wound that will pass with time. I had a soldier patient in the Philippines who had the same kind of an injury. He came out of it. He had been hit in a bolo fight."

"Of course," she said. That was all. Her voice remained ice-cold, without emotion, putting the same great distance between them. She did not believe him. Worse than that, she felt, like her father, that he was responsible.

Lily Ling was the first to move, breaking the spell that held the staring outlaws. She came swiftly to Ellen Sloan's side. "I am here, Miss Sloan," she said. "I will help you. I will be with you."

Frank spoke to Haskell. "Likely all she needs is rest and attention. I must see what I can do for her. At once."

Haskell came to life. "Not by a jugful, Doc!" he said. "She kin walk at least, an' fer all I know she might be fakin' this thing."

He moved close to Ellen, flailing his fists threateningly in her face. She seemed to sense his purpose, for she edged back a pace. But she did not blink. Her eyes remained blank, unseeing.

Haskell was defeated. "Anyway, she kin wait," he said. "We got a couple o' boys that are sufferin' an' need help right now. What difference does it make? She's still Money-bags Sloan's daughter, blind or not blind."

"You did not know Miss Sloan was blind, did you?" Lily Ling cried, anger overcoming her fears. "But I know why you have kidnaped her. You want to use her to set your worthless son free so that he won't be hanged, which he deserves. But why am I here? I am only a penniless Chinese girl. My parents are poor. They could not pay enough ransom to interest you. I own nothing more than the clothes on my back. What is it you want of me?"

It was Hong Kong, the half-caste, who answered that. He pointed toward the tent into which the Chinese woman had retreated. "She is my woman," he said. "She asked me to bring a woman who could be with her when the time comes. She will let only a woman care for her and her baby when it is born. It is her modesty."

Lily Ling seemed to find a measure of strength in that discovery. She stood straighter, prouder. "I see," she said. "So I am worth something, at least, to you scoundrels. I will look after Miss Sloan and be happy to do it. But what if I do not care about your woman or your child?"

"We'll see to that," Haskell said. "You'll do as you're told, like the doc here."

He spoke to his followers. "Clear out a tent fer the Sloan gal and the chink. Don't jest stand there gawkin'. As fer you, chink gal, you'll look after Hong Kong's woman whenever she needs you."

He pushed Frank in the direction of the tent toward which they had been originally heading. "Step lively, Doc," he commanded. "You've got more important work to do than playin' midwife."

Frank spoke to Lily Ling. "See that Miss Sloan rests. I'll bring something so that she will sleep. Have some of these men bring cloths or towels and cold water. Keep cold compresses over her eyes and around her head. Do you understand, Miss Sloan? You must rest, first of all, and follow instructions. I'll come to take a look as soon as possible."

"I understand," Ellen Sloan said.

Haskell pushed Frank determinedly away and into a tent. The flaps were open, the side walls lifted to admit air. Two injured men lay on rude bunks among soiled, wrinkled sheets.

CHAPTER 6

The odor of whiskey was strong in the air, and Frank surmised it was being used as an opiate. It was evident that both men carried bullet wounds and were suffering. Makeshift bandages had been used.

Frank moved to the side of the nearest man. He was young, no more than nineteen, with stringy, carrot-hued hair and thin, unattractive features. His sunken eyes burned with fever. A matted bandage of torn strips of sheet had been crudely placed around his right leg.

"Bullet in the laig," Haskell said. "We dug out the slug, an' figured it wouldn't amount to much, but Denny has got worse. That laig don't look so good. Neither does he. Let's see what you kin do, Doc."

The other patient was older, with hard features and bushy dark hair. "If'n you're a real doctor, git busy an' give me somethin' so I'll quit hurtin'," he spat.

The man had a bandage around his left shoulder. "You don't act like you're goin' to die very soon," Frank said. "Not in bed, at least. Maybe at the end of a hang rope."

Bart Haskell's guffaw drowned out the profane answer from the wounded outlaw. "The doc's read yore brand, Blackie," Haskell chortled.

Frank opened his medical kit and brought out instruments. He first cut away the bandage on the leg of the younger ruffian. He had trained himself to show no emotion, for he had learned that patients watched him closely, trying to determine from any change of expression in his face the seriousness of their plight.

He had to use considerable will power in this case. The young outlaw's leg was frightfully swollen, and Frank feared that gangrene might already have set in. The bullet had done cruel damage to flesh and muscle, but he believed, although he could not be sure, that the bone had not been touched. From the pallor in Denny's skin much blood had been lost.

"How long ago did this happen, and was a tourniquet used, and for how long?" he asked Haskell.

"Denny stopped that slug three—no, four days ago," the leader said after counting it off on his fingers. "He fixed the tourniquet himself, but I made him loosen it from time to time till we got him here. After all, I know somethin' about bullet wounds too, Doc."

He bent close so that he could whisper in Frank's ear. "He's got to lose that laig, I reckon, hey, Doc?"

Denny, who had apparently been in a stupor of pain, heard that. He aroused, his eyes suddenly desperate. "No, you don't!" he choked. "I ain't goin' to be crippled fer life. I'd rather die. You hear that, man? If'n you're a doctor don't you try to cut off my laig. I tell you I'd rather croak."

"Take it easy," Frank said. "Nobody has said anything about the need for cutting off legs or dying. Your kind don't die easy, unfortunately."

"You keep on makin' cute remarks about people like us," Bart Haskell warned, growing ugly, "an' you'll find out it's easy to die—sudden."

Frank knew he was in for a grim task. The tent was small and in disorder. The sun was beginning to make its authority felt on the canvas close overhead, warning of the real onslaught of heat that was coming.

He stripped off his shirt. Haskell peered at him in

surprise. "Say, now at a close look, you don't stack up as poorly as I figgered," he said. "I picked you as a bean pole at about one-sixty. Yo're bigger'n that. I say one-eighty, an' it looks like most of it is muscle. No wonder that jigger you leveled at Pima Flat found out he'd chawed off more'n he could swaller. You didn't git them biceps walkin' around sickbeds in hospitals, now did you?"

Frank didn't bother to answer. "Fetch something that can be used as an operating table," he said. "And water. Cold water will do in this heat. Pans and a bucket that can be thrown away. There's pollution in at least one of these men that must be drained. I'll need bandages, plenty of bandages. There's no time to waste. Get moving!"

Haskell glared, scowling at being ordered around, but he began shouting instructions. The camp swarmed with activity.

Denny reached out with feverish fingers and gripped Frank's arm. "I heard what you said, Doc," he said faintly. "An' *you* heard what I said. I meant it. Don't try to cut off my laig. If'n you do, an' I have to go through life a cripple, I'll hunt you down—damned if I won't—an' kill you."

"You'll likely have to stand in line," Frank said. "You're the second man in only a day who's promised to shoot me."

"Who?" Denny asked.

"His name is Henry Sloan," Frank said. "You probably wouldn't know him by sight, but that's his daughter out there."

Planks and improvised sawhorses were brought in to serve as an operating table.

One of the outlaws opened a case of new, unused cotton sheets. "Compliments o' the railroad," he said, grinning. "It furnishes us with most everything a man could ask fer—free. Jest name whatever else you might need, Doc, an' we'll likely have it if we search around. There're barrels an' boxes we ain't even looked at yet."

Frank tore a strip from one of the sheets, formed a pad, and drew a bottle from his case. He removed the cap and poured a small quantity of a sweet-smelling liquid on the pad.

"Take a whiff," he said, preparing to hold the pad to Denny's face.

"What's that stuff?" Denny demanded, recoiling.

"Just a little touch of ether to bring sweet dreams," Frank said.

Denny found the strength to push Frank's hand away. "Oh no, you don't!" he gasped. "Yo're tryin' to put me to sleep so you kin cut off my laig. I ain't lettin' you."

"It's your choice," Frank said. "Stay awake and suffer, or sleep and dream. However, I promise you I won't do anything drastic unless you know about it. Now take a whiff."

Denny tried to refuse, but did not have the will to make the choice. He sank back, breathed the anesthetic, and his eyes closed. Frank used his stethoscope. The young outlaw was very weak, racked by fever and loss of blood. There was a chance his heart might stop.

Frank worked swiftly. Selecting a scalpel from his case, he lanced Denny's swollen leg. Lily Ling entered the tent at that moment. "Miss Sloan is lying down," she began. "Can I be of any help, Doctah? I will try."

Both she and Haskell turned sickly green, and Frank feared that he might have other patients on his hands. But the Chinese girl steadied, clenched her teeth, and applied herself rigidly to following his orders. Haskell fled into the open air.

After a time Frank turned to the other wounded outlaw. Blackie's injury offered much less of a problem. The man had been hit at the back of the shoulder by a bullet that had torn through flesh and apparently had grazed the shoulder blade. Blackie's tough body was more than holding its own in spite of the haphazard care that had been given the injury.

"Unfortunately you'll be up and around in a few days," Frank said. "How fast were you running when the bullet overtook you?"

"I don't take kindly to people what talk to me like that," Blackie snarled.

Frank turned back to his other patient. He had feared there would be no alternative to amputating the young outlaw's leg, but after finishing draining and cleansing the injury as best he could, he believed there was an even chance in favor of Denny retaining his leg. Gangrene had not yet set in.

He drew from his case a brown bottle which contained small crystals, some of which he dissolved in a basin of water. He used the solution on the wounds of both men and on the dressings he applied.

"What's the stuff?" Bart Haskell inquired. He had overcome his repugnance enough to return to the open flap of the tent.

"Chloral hydrate," Frank said.

"That don't mean nothin' to me," Haskell said. "I never was much on them ten-dollar words you people toss round. But I got a feelin' I've seen it somewhere."

"I wouldn't be surprised," Frank said. "There's another name for it. Knockout drops."

"What? Say, yo're right. I knew I'd seen that stuff before. But what'n blazes are you usin' knockout drops on Denny an' Blackie fer?"

"Doctors have other uses for it than people who put a few drops in the drinks of drunken men so that they can be robbed in a back alley," Frank said. "I take it that is where you became acquainted with chloral hydrate. I'm sure every cheap saloon and bawdy house has a supply of it on hand. But it can also be used as an antiseptic. I'm short on other and better forms of the drug, so I'm falling back on that to hope it will help drive away infection."

"Well, well," Haskell said. "Chloral what-you-call-it, hey? Now ain't that somethin'? A doctor carryin' knockout drops around with him. You learn something every day."

Frank completed the bandaging, arranged the contents of his medical case, and snapped the lid shut.

Haskell picked up the case. "I'll take care o' this, Doc," he said. "You'll git it whenever you need it. There air some toys in it that you might find use for, an' not on Denny or Blackie. Such as them knives an' saws. I don't want you to git any ideas about leavin' us sudden-like."

"I'll need it a while longer," Frank said. "I want to take a look at Miss Sloan."

"Then I'll just tag along an' watch," Haskell said. "I ain't too sure but what you two are runnin' a high blaze on me an' that she ain't as blind as you pretend."

Frank felt utterly spent and helpless. All the stress and strain of the past hectic hours came upon him.

Lily Ling gazed at him anxiously. "You must rest, Doctah!" she said.

He tried to laugh chidingly at her, but his swollen lips would not respond. His attempt at amusement ended in a croak. "Don't try to treat me like I'm an old man," he said.

Denny was beginning to mumble and moan. The effects of the ether were wearing off. "After a while you can have him lifted back on his bed," Frank told Haskell. "And get rid of this table. I won't need it—for the time being at least."

He and the Chinese girl left the tent, followed by Haskell. They made their way to a tent a distance away in the scattered camp. Ellen Sloan lay on a cot in the tent which evidently had been hurriedly vacated by its former outlaw occupants and refurnished with new cots and fresh sheets from the generous supplies the outlaws had on hand.

She was not asleep, however. Frank lifted the damp compress Lily had formed for the patient. He opened his medical kit and examined her eyes through his surgical magnifying glass. She endured the inspection without speaking and with the same remoteness that told him she seemed determined to share her father's attitude toward him. He not only met a stone wall as far as her thoughts went, but also as to the cause of her blindness. The wound across her temple seemed so minor. It was continuing to heal normally.

He drew from his case a sedative in powder form, the last he happened to have. "I'll need a cup of water," he told Haskell. The man bawled an order, and one of the outlaws soon arrived with a filled tin cup.

At the same moment Hong Kong also came at a run to look into the tent. He pointed at Lily Ling. "Come, you!" he barked. "My woman needs you. She believes her time has come."

Lily shrank from him and turned appealingly to Frank. "I would like for you to go with me and see this woman," she said. "After all, this is something I know nothing about."

"No!" Hong Kong exclaimed. "Not him. My woman does not want it. It is not decent. She wants only this girl to help her. This is why I brought her here."

Frank saw that it was useless to debate the point. He gave Lily what instructions he could. "But, mainly, let nature take its course," he said. "If there is trouble, call out, and I will tell you what to do. If you think I should take a hand I will do so—if possible."

The woman's stifled scream came from the tent in the distance. Hong Kong seized Lily's arm and ran, hurrying her to the aid of the patient who was in labor.

Frank mixed the sedative. "Drink this," he said to Ellen Sloan.

She at first would not drink of the cup that he held to her lips. "What is your diagnosis?" she asked.

He felt that it would be useless with this girl to attempt anything but a direct answer. "I'm not sure," he said. "I don't know what to think."

"You're supposed to be a doctor—remember?" she said.

"Or a hoodlum who goes around starting gun fights," he replied curtly.

"You believe I will always be blind," she said.

"On the contrary I believe this may only be temporary," he said, and he tried to be convincing. "A paralyzed optic nerve, most likely, that will respond in time. The only cure I want to try now is rest and quiet for you. Drink this and you will sleep. I'm hoping that is all you need."

"And if it doesn't work?"

"Then we'll have to try something else," he said.

"You mean—operate?"

"No," Frank said. "Not here, at least. In the first place I would not have the equipment, even if I was qualified for such a job, which I'm not. I am better at hammer-and-tongs surgery."

"Such as taking care of thugs who were shot trying to commit a crime," she said.

"Would you prefer that I let them die?"

She made a sudden apologetic gesture. "I am sorry I said that, or even thought of it. But—but lying here waiting while you attended them was not the easiest moment of my life. I'm afraid I'm not resigned to what they have done or what they intend to do with—with all of us."

"There are specialists who can do wonders in nerve and optical surgery," he said. "I know one in particular in San Francisco. You may have heard of him also. Dr. Elias Burke. I can recommend him highly."

Her lips framed a small, bitter, brief smile that faded as quickly as it had formed. "None of us will live to leave this place," she said. "You know that. Lily Ling knows it. Worse than that, if either of us should be allowed to leave, it will not be Lily or you. You both know that also. No, Lily has not said that to me. But she knows. You and she have seen their faces. You could identify them later. But me . . ."

She shrugged it away. "Drink this," Frank said and again held the cup to her lips. This time she drank, grimacing a little at the tart, bitter taste of the potion.

"You will sleep now," Frank said. "I'll be around in case you need anything."

She managed to form a sardonic smile and pointed in the direction of Bart Haskell, who had stood by, watching and listening. "That's the one who calls himself Jesse James, isn't it?" she said. "I know he's there, for he always smells of whiskey. He's the one who brought me here so I could be traded for the release of his son from jail."

"Stop talking and go to sleep," Frank said, realizing that she was fading into a fantasy land of dreams. "My—my father will kill you, Doctor," she mumbled. "He will kill you on sight. He would have killed you when he learned I was blind. But—but I didn't tell him. I didn't want him to—to be—a—murderer."

She drifted off, her voice fading.

Frank waited for a few moments to be sure Ellen Sloan had really fallen asleep. Haskell picked up the medical kit and said, "Come on! She's out, Doc."

Outside the tent, Haskell cocked an eyebrow at him and said, "So now you know?"

"Know what?" Frank asked.

"Ag'in I tell you to quit playin' cute—or dumb with me. You heard just what she told you. Old Moneybags Sloan will kill you on sight. He'd have done it right back there at Pima Flat if he'd known that you was the cause o' his daughter goin' blind. She saved yore bacon that time by not lettin' him know. But he'll soon know."

"How?"

"Never you mind that, Doc. I know about everythin' thet goes on hereabouts and in a hurry. In the first place saw-bones like you don't rate much above coyotes in Henry Sloan's book. Maybe you heerd about how he blamed some quack or other for the deaths of his wife an' young son some years back. Since then he's never had any truck with you pill-pushers. An' he'll have a danged sight less now that he holds you responsible fer his daughter bein' blind."

"No man in his right mind would act that way," Frank said.

"Nobody ever accused Moneybags Sloan o' bein' in his right mind when he felt thet he had a score to pay," Haskell said. "Now, whar do you want to throw down yore tarp an' blankets?"

Frank glanced around. The shade of the tent where Ellen Sloan and Lily Ling had been placed offered the best shelter. "Right here," he said. "I want to be handy in case I'm needed."

Haskell frowned, not liking the idea, then shrugged. "All right." He began shouting orders, and presently some of his followers came dragging, of all things, a mattress, along with sheets and pillows.

Haskell grinned. "We live in style here. You've earned a good rest, Doc. We'll talk things over later on. I'm a little short of shut-eye myself. Pleasant dreams, an' keep out of that tent unless I'm present. I don't want no secret palaverin' goin' on with you an' the Sloan girl or the chink."

Frank settled down on the bed close to the wall of the tent beyond which Ellen Sloan slept. From the distant tent where Lily Ling had gone to the aid of the Chinese woman came the occasional, spaced outcries of the expectant mother. Frank counted them, then settled down to catch what sleep he could.

CHAPTER 7

Frank had slept less than an hour when he awakened. The outcries were coming regularly from the tent where the Chinese woman lay. The outlaws around the eating table were pretending not to hear, but they had stopped all action and were drinking heavily. They were listening in spite of themselves.

Frank had heard screams of pain before, too many times, but little of it had come from the birth of a new life. The great majority had issued from the lips of mangled, injured men. The eyes of all of them were burned deep in his memory. Those eyes had implored him to save them even as death was taking them. Denny's eyes had been like that. Even Ellen Sloan's eyes had reflected that hope. In some cases that faith in him had been rewarded, but the successes had been all too few when balanced against the failures.

Another sound came. It was the thin, protesting outcry of a newborn baby. The screaming of the Chinese mother ended. The tension broke in the outlaw camp. The ruffians burst into wild laughter. They began cavorting around, slapping each other on the backs, hurling hats in the air.

"You're a papa, Hong Kong!" they bellowed. They caught the pudgy half-caste and roughed him up. He was grinning, embarrassed. A new keg of whiskey was broached.

Bart Haskell was not taking part in the celebration. He

stood in the open flap of his tent, which was the largest in camp and obviously the most comfortably equipped. His thumbs were hooked in the sagging belt that supported his holstered six-shooter and there was scorn in his eyes as he watched his rollicking followers.

He sauntered to where Frank was standing, smiling sardonically. "Maybe you was kind of thinkin' that you could take to the hills while the boys was busy, hey, Doc?" he asked.

Frank surveyed the surroundings. An attempt to escape in broad daylight was obviously out of the question. There was little or no cover for several hundred yards in all directions. Beyond rose the labyrinth of ridges stained red and brown by oxidation, and the sterile crests of the dunes.

"As a matter of fact I was thinking of it," he told Haskell. "All I need are wings."

"Correct," Haskell said. "Yo're smart enough to know you wouldn't have a chance. There's only one way out, an' it's guarded, even if you happened to find it, which would take some doin'. So take it easy. We need you. Yo're here to look after Denny and Blackie. I'll do the lookin' after of the Sloan gal. An' the Chinese gal too. As fer you—"

He paused, turning to gaze upward. Frank peered. A small bright light was flashing from a ridge far above the oasis. Frank realized that it was a heliograph, a common form of communication that was used by the army as well as by railroad construction and survey parties. A message was being flashed.

Haskell stood watching intently, his lips moving. He was reading the code. He began to grin. As the flashing ended he lifted a clenched fist in a gesture of triumph. The horseplay had ended at the mess table as the men realized that the heliograph was in operation.

"What'd Whitey say, Bart?" one of them demanded eagerly. "What'd he say?"

Evidently Haskell was the only one of the gang who was versed in the helio code. However, Frank had picked up some knowledge of that form of communication while in the Philippines, enough so that he had managed to read the gist of the message.

Haskell was not keeping the news a secret. "We done it!" he shouted and threw his hat on the ground in triumph. "They're already turned Clem loose. Whoopee!"

The outlaws once more erupted into gleeful shouting and cavorting. Some came to pound Haskell on the back, obviously anxious to flatter him so as to curry favor.

Frank could see that Haskell understood this, for the contempt was deeper in his face, although he pretended to smilingly accept the praise. It was apparent that Haskell felt that he owed no loyalty to his followers, and Frank decided that, in fact, he did not really trust any of them. They were typical criminals, childish of thought and deed, who would spend the greater parts of their lives behind bars, or would die at the hands of some law officers. They lacked the intelligence to plan really profitable crimes, being more of the back-alley slugging element. They needed a leader who possessed the cunning they lacked, a man who could visualize all the pitfalls of a potential crime as well as the rewards, and judge whether one balanced out the other. Apparently Haskell, despite his rough exterior, met that standard, at least in contrast to the ability of the majority of his followers.

However, Frank had the impression that Haskell had lost considerable face, and was on probation because of the disastrous outcome of the attempt to rob the bank in San Bernardino. More and more he believed there was an undercurrent of dissension in the camp, and that the burly Pete Mace was at the bottom of it. However, he also believed Haskell was capable of coping with it and with Pete Mace.

Haskell apparently understood the mental caliber of his cutthroats. He made a point of dressing no better than they and of being no smarter. That, Frank decided, was a measure of self-protection so that he would be in a position to merge into the crowd if trouble came and could take care of himself much better than they, no doubt.

He peered toward the ridge. He could make out the tiny figure of a man on foot there. The man was moving to a higher point south of the position from which the message had been flashed, and soon was out of sight. He was the heliograph operator, and evidently also operated as a lookout from a higher point where he probably could view miles of the route by which Haskell had led his outlaws and captives into the hide-out.

He discovered that Haskell was watching him closely. "Do you savvy blinker talk, Doc?" the outlaw demanded.

"Me?" Frank responded. "It's all gibberish to me. How did that fellow up there—I heard them call him Whitey—find out what was going on in San Bernardino?"

Haskell could not resist boasting. "Me an' Whitey an' another one of the boys used to be in the United States Signal Corps together. The other boy is down on the desert where he's got water wells an' raises hay an' runs a few cattle. He's tapped in on the railroad telegraph line. When he gits any news fer us, he rides up into the hills a piece where he's got a blinker hid out that's in view of Whitey, an' sends the word along to us."

He waited for Frank's praise and Frank accommodated him. "Clever. Very smart."

"I'll say," Haskell agreed. "It took me well on to three years to git this setup workin', but it's unbeatable. Now we're gittin' set to really cash in on it. We're about through with petty stuff like robbin' box cars an' stickin' up mule skinners."

Because of the success of his present plan, Haskell was in a glowing talkative mood and Frank took advantage of it. "So that's how you knew Henry Sloan's daughter was on that train last night," he said.

"Yeah!" Haskell said. "He'd sent telegrams two, three days ago to business people in Berdoo thet he was comin' home. I first aimed to take him, but when I found out his daughter was along I changed plans, figurin' it'd be easier to git Clem free that way. I had wrote a letter beforehand, tellin' the sheriff I'd trade off ol' Moneybags fer my son. But I rewrote it after we left Pima Flat as we were ridin' along an' left it in the coach whar it couldn't be overlooked. I addressed it to Jim Driscoll an' told him to let my son go if Henry Sloan wanted to see his daughter alive ag'in."

"And you will let her go now that they've turned your son loose?" Frank asked.

Haskell glared angrily at him, not liking the question. "O' course," he finally said. He added quickly, "But not till Clem walks into this camp free an' unhurt. I don't trust Jim Driscoll. An' I don't trust Moneybags Sloan even half that much."

The man was lying. Frank was suddenly coldly certain that Ellen Sloan was no nearer freedom than she had been before the heliograph had flashed its message.

He said nothing, for Haskell was still studying him intently, undoubtedly trying to read his thoughts. Pity for Ellen Sloan ran deeply in him. Blind, helpless to protect herself, he could picture her plight with these men. Lily Ling's situation was equally desperate.

He wheeled abruptly, leaving Haskell standing there. He

was sure the outlaw's eyes were following him. Haskell would be certain, of course, that he would be planning to escape, planning it every moment, every minute. Haskell had seen evidence at Pima Flat that Frank was physically capable of taking care of himself, and was dangerous. In addition, Frank was educated, an advantage Haskell lacked, and which he respected in spite of himself. But his greatest apprehension was that Frank's intelligence might be more than a match for his own.

Frank walked to the tent where the two wounded outlaws lay. The stolid heat of the day was adding to their misery. He called for his medical kit, which Haskell sent in the hands of a gangling, snag-toothed, wolfish-faced outlaw who resented being treated as a messenger boy.

"What name do you go by?" Frank asked.

"Me?" the man sneered. "I'm Cole Younger. I reckon you've heard plenty about me."

"Nothing I'd repeat in decent company," Frank said. "Cole Younger has been dead for years. What's your real name?"

"I jest told you my name," the man snarled.

Blackie uttered a snort of derision from his pallet. "The doc knows the real names of me an' a lot of the rest of us," he said. "He might as well know yores. This long-legged polecat is Luke Clay, an' he's such a low-down thief there ain't even a bounty on his head, at least enough to interest any law dog into takin' the trouble to look fer him. Cole Younger likely turns over in his grave every time he hears this leppie use his name."

Luke Clay flew into a rage. Cursing, he could have leaped bodily on the wounded man, but Frank moved in, seized him, and hurled him out of the tent. Luke Clay scrambled to his feet and started to draw his six-shooter. But he thought better of it when he glanced toward Bart

Haskell, who was watching from a distance. Haskell's hand was already on the handle of his own six-shooter. Clay went stumbling away, mumbling threats. He rejoined the group who were still drinking and celebrating the birth of the child.

Frank took Denny's temperature and used the stethoscope. The young outlaw, his eyes still burning with fever and fear, watched with straining desperation. "What's it to be, Doc?" he finally demanded. "You ain't still thinkin' of takin' off my laig, are you?"

"I'll let you know one way or another by tomorrow, maybe sooner," Frank said. "It's fifty-fifty right now, I'd say."

"No, it ain't!" Denny rasped. "There's goin' to be no fifty-fifty about it." He produced a six-shooter from some hiding place about his pallet, clicked the cylinder with a thumb. "I told you I'd kill you, Doc, if you try it," he said. "Fix up that laig so I can walk again. You hear me?"

He meant it. He rocked back the hammer, and Frank found himself staring into the maw of the gun—into the face of death. The youth was half delirious.

"Go ahead," Frank said. "Pull the trigger. Then we'll both die. Without me you haven't got a chance, Denny."

Blackie, on the opposite pallet, had lifted his head, and was staring. The man's evil face bore an expression of savage anticipation. He wanted to be entertained by bloodshed.

Denny slowly lowered the gun and thrust it out of sight. Blackie's head fell back, and he uttered a grunt of disappointment. "You never did have sand in yore craw, Denny," he sneered.

"Maybe I saved your life too," Denny mumbled. "After all, the doc is takin' care o' that hole in your carcass as well as the one in mine."

Frank examined Blackie. For the only time in his career as a doctor he found that he had no real interest in whether his patient lived or died, but he had never wavered in the oath he had taken when he had received his medical degree that his training be used for the benefit of mankind without fear or favor, without prejudice of race or religion.

Blackie must have seen the dislike in him. The man scowled and said, "I've got a gun handy too, fella. Don't go to treatin' me like I was a piece of dog meat that wasn't worth worryin' about. I warn you that I git out of this bed sound an' well or I'll hold you fer it. Denny might be a lump of putty, but Blackie Burns is cut from a tougher piece of whang leather."

Denny spoke hastily. "He means it, Doc, jest like I do. Don't rile him. He's a swift. Real handy with a six. Killed three or four fellers that thought they was pretty fancy on the draw."

"Were they looking at you when you shot them?" Frank asked Blackie.

"Keep pushin', fella, an' you'll find out," Blackie raged.

"Your mother must be proud of you," Frank replied.

He did what he could for the two men. Blackie was in no danger and should be up and around in a day or two, but Denny's situation was a different matter. The young outlaw was wavering between life and death. Denny must have read that bitter truth in Frank's face in spite of his effort to maintain a professional calm. The young outlaw uttered a moan, and began to sob. "I'm a goner, ain't I?" he wept.

"Quit sniveling," Frank said. "You're not dead yet."

He left the sick tent and returned to his place alongside the tent that housed Ellen Sloan. She heard him arrive and came to the flap. She still wore the damp compress like a turban over her forehead and eyes.

"Is that you, Dr. Conroy?" she asked. "What happened?

I heard all the celebrating after the baby was born. Lily is still with the mother. But something else took place. I heard them yelling like wild men."

Frank debated for an instant whether to explain, then realized it would only be cruel to keep the truth from her. "Word came that Haskell's son has been released in San Bernardino," he said. "They've got a heliograph system set up, and they have the telegraph line tapped along the railroad somewhere, so that they can get news into this place quick and fast—in daytime, at least."

She was silent a moment as though dreading to ask the question that was paramount in her mind. "Does that mean that I—we will be turned loose?"

"That was the deal," Frank said. "Haskell told me he would wait until he saw his son safe and free."

"Do you believe he will keep his word?" she asked slowly.

"Of course," he said.

She did not speak for a moment. "No," she finally spoke. "You really don't believe it. Nor do I. He's lying. He has some other plans for—for us."

"Now whatever put such thoughts in your mind?" Frank asked quickly, not daring to hesitate, knowing that would only help confirm her belief. "Of course he'll turn you loose. Whatever else would he want to hold you here for?"

She did not answer that. "When will Haskell be sure his son has been really freed?" she asked.

"As I understand it Bart seems to think that the rascal is expected to show up at this hide-out as fast as he can get here. How soon that might be I can't guess."

"Can he not be trailed?"

"I doubt if they will try," Frank said.

"But why? But—" Then she understood. "Oh, I see. You believe they fear it might endanger my life."

"Of course there's always the chance they might try it," Frank said. "Evidently no white man knows about this oasis, and the Indians are said to be superstitious about coming into the Playground. In addition, Haskell has a lookout on a ridge who likely can warn them in case of danger. And that narrow slit we followed for so long in reaching this place seems to be very hard to locate."

With a weaker person he might have tried to gloss over the situation, but, more and more, he was learning of the great strength of character in Ellen Sloan. She gravely considered what he had said, but she was not quailing, and there was no sign of her breaking down or despairing.

"Thank you," she said.

"For what?" he asked.

"For telling me the truth. For not treating me as the burden that I am."

Lily Ling came to the tent. She was wan, worn after the ordeal of the child's birth. Ellen Sloan seemed to sense the Chinese girl's need for solace. She opened her arms and Lily Ling rushed into them, and began sobbing out her story of responsibility and travail.

"That awful, awful woman," she moaned. "She said she would kill me if things did not go right with her. She does seem to care about the baby, however. I do not want to go back there. But I must."

"The baby will be all right and so will the mother," Ellen Sloan said soothingly. "Is it a girl?"

"A boy," Lily said bitterly. "Another outlaw to prey on the world. And I helped bring him into that world."

"It's high time for you to have some real rest," Frank said, adopting a brusque professional tone. "And Miss Sloan could do with some more. I'll be close around in case of need."

He returned to his mattress, moving it to a new place in

the shade of the tent. Silence came from the two girls and he decided that they had both followed his orders and were asleep. And he also slept once more.

It was sundown when he awakened. Heat lay torpidly over the camp. The majority of the outlaws were asleep, sprawled on pallets in the tents and shacks, with walls open to any breeze that stirred. One of them, wearing a stained cook's apron, was touching a match to wood in the cookstove and another was sullenly peeling potatoes at the mess table, preparing the evening meal.

An outlaw lolled nearby on a mattress under a rude canvas shelter that had been improvised to ward off the hot sun. He was the snag-toothed Luke Clay whom Frank had manhandled out of the tent of the wounded men earlier in the afternoon. Clay had a six-shooter thrust in his sagging belt.

He glared at Frank with tired animosity. " 'Bout time you was wakin' up," he said. "I was of a mind to do some proddin'. Denny's been callin' fer you."

Frank sat up and began pulling on his brogans. He felt centuries old. He could hardly believe that it had been only the previous day since he and Ramon Zapata had alighted from the work train at Pima Flat.

There was no sound from beyond the wall of the nearby tent, not even the breathing of sleepers, and he surmised that the guard's voice had awakened Ellen Sloan and the Chinese girl.

"Where's Haskell?" he asked.

"Still sleepin' like I'd be if'n he hadn't put me on watch over you," Luke Clay growled. "You wasn't the only one that lost out on shut-eye lately. I ain't had much more'n a dozen winks in two, three days, seems like. Now stir yourself an' git over there to take a look at Denny. He's blastin' with fever. I been pourin' water into him like he was a sieve."

Frank walked groggily to the tent where his two patients lay. Blackie was sitting up, obviously in need of little or no attention. But Denny was bathed in perspiration. He looked at Frank, vast fear in his sunken eyes.

Frank sent Luke Clay to bring his medical case, and started his examination. He finally finished with the thermometer and stethoscope and began redressing Denny's leg.

"What's the verdict, Doc?" Denny finally burst out, his voice thin with apprehension.

"There's no gangrene," Frank said. "The slug knocked off some bone splinters, and that is what's causing the trouble now. They've got to be taken out. I'll tend to it tomorrow after some more of this poison has drained away. It'll hurt a little but I'll put you asleep for a spell."

"You—you think I got a chance?" Denny asked hoarsely.

"You might make it now," Frank said.

Denny eyed him suspiciously, torn between sudden wild hope and black doubt. "You wouldn't lie to me, would you, Doc?" he demanded. He moved suddenly and Frank once more found himself staring into the muzzle of a six-shooter. Denny had lifted it from its hiding place.

"As far as I'm concerned, you're not worth lying to, Denny," Frank said. "Don't you know that it's dangerous to play with firearms?"

Denny started to resent that, then ruled against it. Hope began to overcome his doubts. "You got plenty of grit, Doc," he said with grudging admiration. "I'm beginnin' to believe yo're tellin' the truth an' that I might not lose my laig."

"Don't get me wrong," Frank said. "You're a long way

from being on the safe side, but we'll know for sure, one way or the other, by tomorrow. Lie quiet. Do what I tell you and there's a chance you might even be around on crutches in a few days."

He closed the medical case, which Luke Clay quickly appropriated. Leaving the tent, he found Haskell waiting. The outlaw leader wore an ugly, wicked grin. He held in his hand rusty leg shackles of a type from past generations. They consisted of iron bands, made to clamp with a key around a prisoner's ankles, with a short length of connecting chain that would hobble the wearer.

"Set down, Doc," Haskell said, indicating a nearby bench. "I've got a present fer you. Bracelets. It's because I think so much of you I don't want you to git any notions of leavin' us sudden-like."

He pushed Frank down on the bench and clamped the bands on his ankles. The shackles were heavy. The chain clanked as Frank arose and tested the arrangement. He could take only short, measured steps. Running would be out of the question.

"I'm touched," Frank said. "I didn't know how valuable I was to you."

"So now you know," Haskell smirked.

Frank hobbled to his place at the tent occupied by the girls. Lily Ling appeared in the flap, her eyes widening in horror and pity as she saw the shackles. Ellen Sloan was at her side, and Frank saw new despair in her as Lily told her what had happened.

The same despair bore heavily on Frank. There had been a momentary ray of desperate hope in his mind when Denny had again produced his six-shooter from its hiding place. The thought of trying to gain possession had raced through his mind in spite of the odds that were so heavily banked against him. Now the shackles had lengthened even those odds.

Escape! Escape! That was the overwhelming issue growing in his mind. It was beginning to possess his thoughts every moment, even though he knew that he could never leave here alone if his own chance should come.

CHAPTER 8

Dusk came, and he was allowed to hobble to the eating table and partake, along with the outlaws, of a greasy stew that was ladled onto tin plates along with hardtack bread, canned peaches, and black coffee that was passed out in the same tin cups the outlaws used for their drinking of whiskey. Dozens of kegs of whiskey were pyramided in the shade of rude shelters, along with cases and barrels and boxes of other food supplies, clothing, and implements, all stolen, no doubt from railroad cars or from army quartermaster depots. It all proved how long the oasis had served as a hide-out for the outlaw organization.

Bart Haskell carried plates of food to the tent where Ellen Sloan and Lily Ling were held. A fresh keg of whiskey had been broached, and the outlaws grew boisterous. One of them arose and began following Haskell, intending to enter the tent with him. Haskell turned, kicked the man viciously in the stomach, sending him pitching to the ground, retching and gasping.

"I tell all of you fer the last time to wait," Haskell yelled, addressing all his followers. "Ever hear o' the goose and the golden egg, an' what happened to it when some fool did away with it? Well, we got a goose that'll lay a lot of gold eggs fer us. Stay away from that tent. I'm the only one that goes into it. You hear me now?"

The outlaws heard. They had been jeering and uttering coarse remarks, but they now subsided into muttering resentment. The man Haskell had kicked got to his feet and slouched sheepishly back to the mess table where he was met by sneers and derision. There was no loyalty, no comradeship among these men. They adhered only to the law of the pack. Frank was sure the two feminine hostages had heard Haskell's statement and understood its significance. They were only relatively safe as long as Ellen Sloan was valuable to the ruffians.

The camp settled down, the outlaws turning their attention to poker-playing and drinking from the broached keg. From the distance came the rhythmic clang of a hammer on the anvil as one of the gang, with forge fire glowing in the dusk, fitted a shoe to one of the horses.

The newborn baby began squawling weakly. The mother shouted, demanding that Lily Ling come to her aid. The Chinese girl appeared reluctantly, gave Frank a despairing look, and headed wearily for the nursery tent.

Bart Haskell had disappeared into his personal tent. In spite of what had happened to his comrade, one of the outlaws took advantage of the chance to defy the leader's orders. He appeared in Lily's path, seized her in his arms, and tried to press his thick lips upon her. He was the swaggering former pugilist, Pete Mace.

Frank had finished his food and was leaving the mess table. "Let her alone," he said.

Pete Mace turned and peered across the twenty-foot space that separated them. Lily Ling, who had been fighting desperately, managed to break free and race on to the tent where the Chinese mother was calling for her.

Pete Mace's small eyes bore a glint of satisfaction. Frank suddenly realized that Mace had acted deliberately to test Bart Haskell's authority over the outlaws.

"Was you talkin' to me, Doc?" Mace asked.

"Who else?" Frank replied.

"I've killed men fer less," Mace said.

"Not if they were looking at you," Frank said. "And not if they had a gun and an even chance to draw."

A sudden, dead silence came over the camp. The watching outlaws stopped drinking and eating. Pete Mace was packing a six-shooter. Murder was in his eyes.

Bart Haskell emerged from his tent. He also had a pistol, but it was drawn and cocked. "Shootin' down the doc wouldn't do you nor any of us any good right now, Pete," he said. "Denny needs him mighty bad. So does Blackie. Don't try to draw. I wouldn't take it kindly."

Pete Mace had overplayed his hand. With Haskell's gun on him he had no chance and knew it. And, as Frank surmised, he had fallen into a trap Haskell had set for him.

"I was only tryin' to run a skeer into him," Mace said. "He's gittin' a little too big fer his britches, tryin' to tell me what to do. If he didn't have them shackles on, I'd have cuffed him around some."

"Now that'd be the thing to do, Pete," Haskell said. "How about takin' him on with fists? It'll be fun fer all of us."

Avid eagerness came into Pete Mace's muddy eyes. Frank guessed that Mace was deciding that if this was Haskell's attempt to humiliate him he would turn the tables.

"Take them shackles off him, Bart," Mace said, "an' you'll have all the fun you want. I'll beat them high an' mighty ways out of him in a hurry. He roughed Luke Clay up some today on top of treatin' all of us like we was dirt an' him too good to even step on us. It'll be him that'll be the dirt when I git through with him."

Bart Haskell was grinning. "Sure, sure," he said. "Yo're absolutely right, Pete. It's high time he was took down a few pegs—if yo're man enough to do it."

Mace swelled up indignantly. "What do you mean, if I'm man enough?"

"That's what we aim to find out," Haskell said. "You been tellin' it how tough you are. What we want to know is whether that's all it is—just talk."

The outlaw leader, still grinning, drew from his pocket the key to the shackles, bent down, and freed Frank's ankles. He straightened and stepped back, swinging the bands by the chain. "Over there beyond the cook tent," he said. "It's more level."

"I don't seem to have any say in the matter," Frank said.

"None at all," Haskell said. "None at all."

The outlaws began buzzing with anticipation. They were athirst for the chance to watch blood flow as long as it was not their own.

Frank looked at Haskell and saw the sardonic twist to the man's grin. Again he understood that this was not so much of a test of fistic ability between himself and Pete Mace as it was a part of the struggle for power, a battle for leadership over the outlaw organization. Willing or unwilling, he had been cast in the role as Haskell's champion in an attempt to have his rival humiliated.

Mace stripped off his shirt. He had huge upper arms and heavy fists. His thick jaw probably could take considerable punishment, but there was flabbiness about his middle—the price of heavy drinking and careless eating.

Frank spoke to Haskell. "What if I win? What's in it for me?"

"I might make you an offer," Haskell said.

"Such as what?"

"Maybe to throw in with us," Haskell said. "We could use a man like you."

"What about them?" Frank asked, indicating the tent in which the two girls were held.

"That's none of yore worry," Haskell snarled. "The only deal I make with you, Doc, is that I won't let Pete stomp you. We still need a sawbones around here. Denny ain't out of the woods yet."

"I take it that anything goes in this fight," Frank said.

"Anything but stompin' an' gougin'," Haskell said.

"All right," Frank said, and headed for the spot Haskell had indicated. The outlaws followed like a swarm of bees. He saw that Lily Ling was watching from the flap of the nursery tent.

He pulled off his shirt and turned to face his opponent—almost too late, for Mace was charging at him, trying to catch him at a disadvantage. He cast aside the shirt and managed to duck in time, butting his head into Mace's stomach. Mace's flailing fists beat heavily on his shoulders.

He rammed both fists into Mace's stomach. They were short jabs, but they drove the bigger man back, gasping. Frank followed him, fists driving, but Mace managed to parry the punches successfully.

Mace tried to clench, so as to take advantage of his superior weight. It was the same tactic Truck Eggers had attempted at Pima Flat and Frank had expected it. He sidestepped, feinted, ducked, and evaded coming to grips. But he took punishment. One of Mace's clubbing fists grazed his chin, another landed solidly on his left arm below the elbow. The arm went partly numb, but he managed to break clear and spar until the damage faded.

Mace was panting, but the blood lust was running high in him, for he felt that he had slowed Frank down. He came in, swinging. That was his mistake. Frank parried a right and countered with a right of his own, for Mace's jaw was wide open. He followed with a left.

The onlookers, who had been howling and dancing

around, shouting encouragement to Mace, went suddenly motionless and silent.

Frank struck again, a right swing, and Mace's flat nose became flatter, almost disappearing into the crimson folds of his face. Mace, badly hurt, tried to hang on. Frank broke that attempt and swung a right and a left again. Pete Mace reeled back, then fell on his face, knocked cold.

Frank, winded, steadied himself on his feet. Bart Haskell was gazing down at Pete Mace, savage satisfaction in his expression. He moved in and toed Mace's body. "Git up an' fight, Pete," he demanded. "Don't quit like the yaller dog thet you are. Wasn't it you that was tellin' it big how you was goin' to take this dude apart?"

Frank looked at the other outlaws. Their attitudes had changed. They were gazing down at the fallen Pete Mace with evil glee and beginning to jeer him. One of the pack had fallen and the others had their fangs bared to finish him.

He bent over Pete Mace. The man was wheezing, and a bloody froth bubbled on his lips. Frank turned him flat on his back and spread his arms. That eased Mace's respiration. The blood was only from the damage that had been done to his features. His breathing responded. Frank arose, looked around for his shirt, and Haskell handed it to him.

"Have I done you favor enough?" he said to Haskell.

Haskell bristled. "What do you mean—favor?"

Frank didn't bother to answer. Haskell knew what he had meant. He had removed a thorn from Haskell's side. Mace had lost face and Haskell would no longer fear challenge for his leadership, from that direction at least.

Frank discovered that had taken more punishment than he realized. He walked to the rude trough that served as a washbasin, but its water had not been renewed lately. He turned to head toward the open water beyond the marsh for a better chance to cleanse away the sweat and dust and blood.

He found himself staggering a trifle. Pain drove through him from his ribs and left arm. Pete Mace had done far more damage to him than had Truck Eggers in the fight at Pima Flat.

Hands caught him and steadied him. "Lean on me, Doctah," Lily Ling said. She supported him, surprising strength in her small, slim body. Ellen Sloan, as usual, was only a pace away, following the Chinese girl by sound.

"Thanks," Frank said. "I need to wash up."

"There is a place," Lily Ling said. "It is not far. The watah is deeper and clean, and the shore is sandy."

Frank let Lily lead him around the marsh, with Ellen Sloan keeping step with them, a hand on the Chinese girl's shoulder. Lily was warning her of any obstacles she might encounter. Frank, his head clearing, saw that Haskell and another of the outlaws were following them.

"Don't git any ideas of tryin' to run away," Haskell warned.

The open pond appeared and Frank waded in to his waist. He ducked his head under and that drove away the last of the cobwebs. He found that Lily was still at his side. She splashed water on him, sluicing away the blood and perspiration. Ellen Sloan had waded into the water also. Their soaked garments clung to their bodies.

Frank managed a grin that was crooked on his lips, which were again beginning to swell. "You splash me and I'll splash you," he said.

Lily was inspecting him with concerned eyes. "You have a bad cut on your right cheekbone," she said. "Worse than the one that man gave you at Pima Flat. And there are one or two others that are not so deep, but need attention."

"There's court plaster in my case," he said. "And salve. That is, if Haskell will loan us the case again."

"I am afraid the bad one must be stitched, Doctah," she said.

He looked at her. She was pale, but determined. "I have never done such a thing, but if you have the material and can tell me how to do it, I will try," she said.

They waded ashore where Haskell and many of the outlaws were waiting. Ellen Sloan broke her silence. "I would like to help you, Lily."

"You help by being with me," the Chinese girl said. "Then I know that I am not alone. Come. We will take care of the doctah in our tent." She spoke to Haskell. "We will need the medical case."

The case was brought at Haskell's order, and they made their way to the girls' tent. A lantern was lighted. Again Haskell could not stomach it when Lily began using the surgical needle and thread to close the gash on Frank's cheekbone. He retreated outside.

Lily's fingers remained firm and sure. Half a dozen stitches were needed, with Frank giving instructions. When the task was finished, he studied the result in the surgical mirror and nodded approval. "Good girl! You ought to be a surgeon yourself. Now the court plaster."

Lily applied the finishing touches. Then he managed to catch her just in time. Now that she had succeeded, she went suddenly limp and ashen and began to sway. He lifted her in his arms and placed her on one of the cots.

"What is it?" Ellen Sloan cried out. "What happened?"

"Lily has fainted," he said. "And no wonder, after all she's been through." He called out to Haskell. "Have water brought. Cold, clean water from the pond."

It arrived in a tin basin, carried by one of the outlaws.

Ellen Sloan pushed Frank aside and used a damp cloth on Lily's forehead and throat, brushing back her hair.

The Chinese girl's eyes drooped open. She looked up into the faces of Frank and Ellen Sloan and smiled a little. "I was again dreaming that I was at home,"

She came back to reality with reluctance. "It was only a dream," she said. "I am sorry." She looked at Frank's damaged face and the strips of court plaster. "You will have more scars," she said sorrowfully.

"That may be an improvement," Frank said.

"Thank you, Dr. Conroy," she said.

"For what?"

"For saving me from that awful man. For—for everything. I know that you and I will never get out of this place alive. We have seen their faces. They will never—" She broke off, and caught Ellen's hand contritely. "Oh, I am sorry. I should not have said such a thing."

"Do not be sorry, Lily," Ellen Sloan said. "It is something I have already said to the doctor. Never, never be sorry for me. Never pity me. Blindness has some compensations. At least I do not have to see the terrible things that are happening or to look at the faces of these scoundrels as you two are forced to do."

She and the Chinese girl huddled together. Frank left the tent and found Haskell waiting with the leg shackles in his hand.

"That isn't necessary," Frank said. "I wouldn't try to leave here without them. There are bonds stronger than what you have in your hand."

"I'll make sure you don't change yore mind," Haskell said. He clamped the iron bands around Frank's ankles and tightened them with the key.

He saw that Frank was watching as he returned the key

to his pocket. He grinned wickedly. "Jest try an' git it, Doc," he said. "That is if you want maybe a broken jaw to carry around, along with a few other complaints, such as nursin' a touch of red-hot iron to the soles of yore feet. We like yore company an' aim to see that you stay with us. Don't you never try to steal this key away from me."

Frank dragged his rude bed nearer the front flap of the tent in which the girls were quartered. A new guard was lolling on the mattress nearby. The outlaws, at Haskell's orders, were taking two-hour spells at watching over the prisoners. "Day an' night," Haskell had stated. "An' if I ketch anybody sleepin', I'll build a fire under him as long as a well rope."

Haskell approached and eyed Frank's new sleeping position, scowling, and trying to make up his mind about whether to object. Finally he decided to accept it.

"Maybe yo're thinkin' of gittin' cozy with the gals yoreself, Doc," he said jeeringly. "Forget it. The same orders go fer you that go fer the rest of us. Keep out o' that tent. An' I hope you sleep sound. There are scorpions, tarantulas, an' sidewinders in these parts."

"And worse," Frank said. "They walk on two legs. How long are you going to keep this up, Haskell?"

"Till I decide different," the man snapped. "An' quit askin' questions."

"Your son has been turned loose from jail," Frank said. "At least that's what you told your buddies. Maybe you weren't exactly telling them the real facts. Maybe things haven't gone like you planned, and you don't want those jugheads to know that you've missed fire once again, like you did on that San Berdoo holdup."

Haskell drove the toe of a boot against Frank's thigh, sending a shock of numb pain through him. "You just can't help askin' fer trouble, kin you, Doc?" he gritted. "In the first place it wasn't my fault we run into trouble in Berdoo. It just happened we hit bad luck when some fool cowboys who wasn't supposed to be in town showed up at the wrong time an' tried to smoke us up. In the second place I didn't miss fire. Clem's loose. He'll be with me before long. Put that in yore pipe an' smoke it."

"Then there's no point in keeping Miss Sloan here any longer, is there?" Frank asked.

"You do keep frettin' about affairs that's none of yore worry, Doc," Haskell raged. "Don't you go tryin' to tell me what to do. It might just happen that I'll decide to keep her around a while longer. After all, Henry Sloan's purty well fixed. He won't miss a few thousand dollars to see his daughter ag'in, alive an' well, if I decide to ask fer it. That'd make up for what we missed in San Berdoo."

Frank realized he had made a mistake in starting this conversation. His original thought had been to allay any suspicions Haskell might hold that he was versed in reading the heliograph. But it was too late now. Ellen Sloan and Lily Ling were undoubtedly listening beyond the thin walls of the tent.

Haskell, with his capacity for torture, knew this also and continued the ordeal. "Old Moneybags Sloan has been a big toad in the pond too long, ridin' around on silver-chased saddles an' fancy palominos. It's my turn to play the fiddle, an' I aim to make him dance to my tune."

Frank sank back on his pallet, turning his back on the outlaw leader in order to end this devastating conversation. Haskell walked away, laughing, pleased with himself. His men were at the mess table, starting their evening session of drinking and poker. Frank waited, hoping against hope that the girls had not fully understood what Haskell had said. But the damage had been done.

Ellen Sloan finally spoke through the tent wall. "I'll

prevail on him to let you and Lily go, Doctor," she said. "I'll promise him more money. As he said, my father is well-to-do."

"Haskell was only trying to worry you," Frank said. "He'll turn us all loose eventually."

After that there was silence from the tent, but he knew his attempt at encouraging them had been a failure. Despite his extreme physical weariness, sleep eluded him. The drinking and loud bickering continued at the mess table. Presently, Haskell sent a new man to replace the outlaw who had stood the past trick as guard over the prisoners. The new sentinel was a tough-faced young desperado who pretended that he was known as Billy the Kid. He did not relish missing the conviviality at the poker table for the boring task of watching over two females and a shackled man.

"Hell, none o' you could git a stone's throw away before you was caught an' brung back," he grumbled, settling down on the mattress beneath the shelter. "This here is a waste o' time."

The night wore along, and the outlaws, one by one, were scattering off to their beds in the tents and shacks, the majority of them staggering drunk. "Billy the Kid" dozed, but whenever Frank moved, a betraying clink of the shackle chain caused him to straighten and reach for the six-shooter he had laid close at hand beside him.

The old moon cleared the peaks and painted black and silver shadows on the oasis. The night was balmy and no blankets were needed at present, although Frank knew that toward morning the customary desert chill would set in. His clothes had long since dried on his body. The usual sirocco had sprung up, moaning above the ridges, but barely touching the camp in the depths. No sound came from inside the tent but Frank doubted that the girls were asleep. Like himself, he felt that they were awake, tortured by the hopelessness of their situation.

A new thought came to Frank, and he rolled it over in his mind for a moment. Finally he spoke to the young desperado and got to his feet. "I better take a look at Denny," he said. "Fetch my medicine case. Haskell's got it and he's still up. There's a light in his tent."

He paid no heed to the outlaw's muttered objection, but hobbled toward the tent where the injured men lay. As a matter of fact he was sure that Denny was sleeping, for he had administered an opiate early in the evening.

But he lighted a lantern, and when "Billy the Kid" arrived with the medical case, he opened it and pretended to examine the young outlaw who was well under the spell of the drug. He had used this trip to the hospital tent as an excuse to delve into his medical case in the hope of helping himself to the bottle of chloral hydrate. But the plan he had in mind, desperate as it had been, evaporated as had all the previous projects for escape that he visualized. The bottle was not there. Haskell must have removed it.

Defeated, he extinguished the lantern and hobbled back to his pallet. The wind grew in strength, and gusts reached the camp, whipping at the tents and shacks. The newborn baby began wailing and the Chinese mother screamed for Lily to come. Lily emerged from the tent.

"Where do you think yo're goin', yalla gal?" the guard demanded. "Let that chink take care of her own brat."

"I must see if I can help," Lily said. "After all, it is only a tiny baby. He did not ask to be born in this awful place."

"Make sure you don't go any farther," the desperado warned. "Not one step beyond that tent. You hear me now?"

Lily hurried away to aid the brutalized mother. "Billy the Kid" got to his feet. He had returned the medical kit to

Haskell's tent, and that tent was now dark. He mumbled something, then left his post and made his way steathily to the deserted mess table. Frank guessed that he was helping himself at the whiskey keg.

Lily had vanished into the nursery tent. Lantern light brightened there as a turned-down wick was lengthened. The wailing of the baby went on, but its volume began to dwindle. Frank sank back on his pallet. He suddenly became alert. He could hear the faint scuff of footsteps approaching, and they did not come from the direction that "Billy the Kid" had gone.

A shadow fell across him and he made out the form of a man looming above him in the moonlight. It was the snag-toothed, savage outlaw, Luke Clay. He towered overhead, and Frank realized that the man had a knife in his hand, and the knife was lifted for a downward stroke.

Luke Clay reeked of whiskey. He was breathing hard, and evidently was in an alcoholic frenzy. He had come to take vengeance on Frank for the indignity he had suffered at Frank's hands during the day. He apparently had been waiting in the shadows for this opportunity. It probably was in his mind that he could get away with murder and deny that he had ever left his bunk.

CHAPTER 9

Just as Luke Clay started his plunge to drive the knife home, Frank seized him by the leg, half rose, twisting, and sent him toppling to the ground. The man, possessed of desperate strength, came to his feet, the knife again lifted. He lunged. Frank's shackles caught on some obstruction, but he managed to roll aside as he fell, and the knife missed, driving into the ground at his side.

Clay fell also from the force of the thrust, but reared to his knees, the knife poised again. Frank was almost helpless, for his shackles were caught in a tent peg and there was little chance of again warding off the blade.

Lily Ling arrived. She had in her two hands a rock as big as her fists which she brought down on Luke Clay's head. The ruffian froze for an instant. The knife fell from his fingers. Then he pitched face down on the ground at Frank's side.

"I have killed him!" Lily breathed, horrified.

Frank freed the chain from the tent peg and bent over the fallen outlaw. Luke Clay was breathing thickly.

"No such luck," he said. "He's more drunk than hurt. He's coming around already. He's the kind that has a thick skull with nothing inside it."

Lily picked up the knife. It was a wicked weapon—a skinning knife with a wide six-inch blade, what was commonly known as a Davy Crockett knife.

"I will keep this," she breathed.

Ellen Sloan was standing in the flap of the tent. "What happened?" she whispered. "What is it, Lily?" Her voice was thin, terrified.

"It was that man, the awful one who looks like an animal," Lily said. "He tried to kill the doctah. He is drunk. I have his knife. I will hide it. We will keep it—for the two of us."

Ellen Sloan understood. "Of course," she said huskily. "For the both of us. Of course."

Frank, a chill in his veins, peered into their faces in the shadowy moonlight—into the delicate golden features of the Chinese girl and the pale, set expression of the white captive. He saw mutual decision and determination there.

"Not that," he said. "It must never come to that."

"It will be for us to decide," Ellen Sloan answered.

"Yes," Lily said. An unspoken pact had been made between them.

Frank dragged Luke Clay's limp body a distance from the tent. The man was beginning to revive, so he abandoned him there and returned to the tent. Looking back, he saw that Clay had got on his feet and was slinking away into the shadows. He vanished just in time, for "Billy the Kid" had appeared from the mess shack and was making his way back to his post, a tin cup in his hand.

"What if they search for the knife?" Frank asked.

"I will pray that they do not find it," Lily said.

"I doubt if that man will say anything about losing it," Ellen Sloan said. "I doubt if anyone but he will try to look for it. He won't dare to let anyone know, and particularly Haskell, where he lost it and how. We all heard Haskell warn them as to what would happen to any who came near this tent without his permission."

"You may be right," Frank said. "But let me keep the knife."

"No," they replied almost in unison.

"You must not think of doing away with yourselves," he argued desperately. "We're all still alive and healthy."

There was no more chance for talk because "Billy the Kid" had heard the rumor of their conversation and had quickened his stride. "What have you three been palaverin' about?" he demanded as he arrived. "What are you up to? You're supposed to be asleep."

"We were discussing the weather," Frank said.

The desperado drew his six-shooter, lifted the muzzle threateningly. "I ought to whup you up some," he growled. He evidently had lingered at the whiskey keg, helping himself to make up for lost time in addition to bringing back another generous potion in the tin cup.

"And what will Haskell say and do if he finds out you left your post to fill yourself with booze?" Frank asked.

The outlaw mouthed profanity and quickly let the matter drop. "Git back in yore beds," he snarled at the girls. "An' you too, sawbones. Yo're too sassy for yore health."

The three captives complied. Frank was successful now in wooing sleep and he did not awaken until daybreak.

Ellen Sloan's assessment of Luke Clay's fear of exposure proved to be accurate. The man was up and around, taking his place among his companions in the breakfast line as the cook ladled out beans and biscuits and pork side. He favored an arm, evidently nursing a strained or sprained wrist or shoulder as a result of his encounter with Frank. He kept his hat firmly on his stringy hair—to conceal a lump, no doubt.

Clay was avoiding Bart Haskell. He was obviously uneasy. Also puzzled. Frank hobbled to the mess line, and when he managed to catch Luke Clay's eye, he drooped an eyelid. The desperado expected Frank to inform Haskell about his transgression, but as time moved along and Haskell continued to be apparently unaware of what had happened, Clay's uneasiness shifted into another direction. He began worrying about the silence of the captives.

Frank added to Clay's problem by giving him additional glances and sly winks, but not in a manner that Clay could regard as friendly. Luke Clay's slow mind began to understand. He was being held in a sort of bondage, forced into silence about the whereabouts of the knife he had lost. He knew that if the truth came out, the least he could expect was a mauling that might not stop short of death at the hands of the outlaw leader.

Frank was satisfied with the situation. However, he also realized its dangers. The captives had a lever that might be used on the snag-toothed ruffian if it became worthwhile. On the other hand, Frank was fully aware that Luke Clay had reason for putting all three of them out of the way in order to protect himself from Haskell's wrath.

The day wore along with Haskell obviously growing more and more on edge, but for another reason. He kept scanning the ridges, but the only action Frank saw from Whitey at the heliograph were brief flashes, indicating that there was nothing to report.

Frank's two patients occupied a great part of his time. Blackie was well on his way to recovery and chafing at being confined to his pallet, but Denny's situation was very much in the balance. The fever persisted and he was in great pain. Frank had about exhausted the scant supply of ether and sedatives in his case. He visited the suffering young desperado hourly during the day and had the guards awaken him at intervals during the nights for the same purpose.

Lily Ling was busy also, being called often to the nursery tent where Mary Wong, which was the name the baby's mother went by, was becoming more and more demanding and intolerant.

Frank could see that Lily was worried after returning from one of her trips to the nursery tent. "How are things going?" he asked.

"I am not sure," she answered. "The baby, it cries very much."

"That sounds normal to me in this weather and in this place," Frank said. "He's got good lungs at least."

"That is the trouble," Lily said. "That awful man, Haskell, is being annoyed by the crying. He has told Mary Wong to keep the baby quiet or he will do it for her. She is frightened."

"Babies cry," Frank said. "It's their only way of notifying the world they need food or attention. I don't believe even Haskell would harm an infant."

"I hope you are right, but Mary Wong does not believe it, and she knows Haskell better than any of us. She is a bad woman, but she cares for her baby. That is about all the good I can say for her. I do not feel anything toward her but fear."

"And how do you feel about the baby?"

She gave him a little, wry smile. "You are cruel to ask such a question. You know that, don't you? The sins of the elders should not be charged against such a tiny thing."

The baby began wailing again, and Lily hurried back to the nursery tent.

A buzz of excitement broke out suddenly among the outlaws. They were on their feet running and shouting. Two riders were approaching the camp, coming from the direction of the maze of draws and dunes that masked the entrance to the oasis.

Bart Haskell did not join in the running, but stood near his tent, grinning and waiting. One of his followers slapped him on the back. "You *did* put it over, Bart!" he screeched. "It's Clem, big as life. They did turn him loose! Looks like they fed him purty good too. You made ol' Henry Sloan toe the chalk. I'll bet he saw to it that the sheriff didn't fool around very many minutes after he lit a fuse under his tail, not with us havin' ol' Moneybags' daughter."

Bart Haskell began moving at a more dignified pace to meet the arrivals. One of them was no more than twenty years old, Frank estimated. He had the same heavy-boned face and frame as Bart Haskell, the same aura of vanity and bravado. There was no doubt that he was the outlaw leader's son.

The other rider was being addressed as Whitey by the outlaws. He was lean and gray-templed, with sharp, foxlike features. He was the lookout and heliograph operator who had come down from the ridge to escort the released outlaw into camp.

Clem Haskell dismounted and clasped hands with his father. "How did they treat you, boy?" the elder Haskell asked.

"Mighty polite, mighty polite," Clem Haskell snickered. "But not till Henry Sloan got to town an' come stampedin' to the jail. He throwed his weight around somethin' fierce, an' I want to tell you, Paw, thet they listened. All the bigwigs of the town come pilin' into the jail. As I understand it you've got Henry Sloan's daughter an' made it plain that you wanted me out of that calaboose, pronto, or else. Is that right?"

"That's about the size of it," the father said.

Clem peered around. "Where is she, Paw?" he asked.

"Come on," Bart Haskell said. He led his son to the tent, drew back the flap, and said, "Take a look."

Clem peered. "Two of 'em!" he exclaimed. "And one's a chink. What's she doin' here?"

"Hong Kong brung her along to look after his woman," Bart Haskell explained. "She happened to be on the train."

"That's the first I heard about her," Clem said. He turned and looked at Frank, who had got to his feet and was standing nearby. "But I take it that this dude is the sawbones who's joinin' up with us. I heard about him."

"Yeah," his father said. "This is Doc Conroy. We brought him along from the train when we grabbed the Sloan petticoat. We needed a doc to look after Blackie an' Denny."

A sly grin was spreading over Clem Haskell's face as he continued to peer at Frank. "Well, well," he said. "Welcome to the outfit. Shake, pal."

He extended a hand, which Frank ignored. "I'm a little particular," he told the outlaw.

"Now, that's no way for one of the bunch to act," Clem snickered.

"It happens I'm not one of you," Frank said. "I just told you I'm particular."

"Now, that ain't what Henry Sloan thinks," young Haskell replied, still grinning. "Take a look at this, pal."

He brought from a pocket a paper that was somewhat the worse for wear. He straightened it and held it so that Frank could read. It was a printed dodger of the kind put out by law officers to be posted for public attention:

$5,000 REWARD!

For information leading to the return
of Ellen Evelyn Sloan, daughter of
Henry Sloan, rancher. She was kidnaped
by a man styling himself as Jesse James

whose real name is Barton Haskell. He leads a gang of dangerous outlaws.

ALSO $5,000 REWARD!

For the capture dead or alive of Frank William Conroy, a medical doctor who is an accessory to the kidnaping of Ellen Evelyn Sloan and is a member of the Barton Haskell gang. He is armed and dangerous.

[signed] Henry Sloan

A picture of Bart Haskell was printed on the poster, but it was one made when the man had been much younger. There was also a picture of Frank on the paper. It was a fairly recent portrait taken by a photographer for the railroad in connection with an advertising campaign.

Frank unbelievingly read the words again. "This is ridiculous," he said. "Why would Henry Sloan believe anything like that?"

Clem Haskell answered gleefully. "I told him so. Paw told me to tell him that."

"*You* told him?" Frank exclaimed. "You mean you talked to Henry Sloan personally? When?"

"I talked to old Moneybags when he came to the hoosegow in Berdoo the other day. He tried to scare me by tellin' what was going' to happen to us if his leetle girl wasn't turned loose after I was let go. I cooled him down plenty by givin' him an idea of what might happen to her if he tried any tricks. I sort of mentioned your name, Doc, an' I might have even pointed out that you, bein' a sawbones, an' one of the bunch, might change her looks so that even her old man might not know her when he saw her—or maybe he wouldn't want to know her. I might have even hinted that you might saw off a finger now and then—a lady finger of course—to send to him as a reminder that we had his daughter."

"How did you know that I was held here?" Frank demanded, stunned.

His burly father answered that. "Hell, Doc, we know everything that goes on. Everything! I got word into that Berdoo jail within hours after you got to this place. You seen that blinker up on the rim, didn't you? It works both ways. I've got a lot of friends in this country. A couple of 'em even wear law badges an' draw county pay. They don't mind earnin' a little extra money by passin' along information. I've got a big organization."

"Nobody would believe this," Frank said, indicating the dodger.

"Henry Sloan believes it," Clem Haskell said. "I told him you'd been workin' with us fer months, tippin' us off as to things bein' shipped on the railroad that might be worthwhile for us to grab. He shore swallered it, hook an' all. He frothed at the mouth. He raved about you bein' in on stealin' his daughter. I don't reckon anybody will ever collect that five thousand he put on your haid, Doc. Henry Sloan will kill you before anybody else gits a chance."

His father was beaming. "Clem's smart," he said. "As smart as me, almost. Keep what he said in mind in case you've still got any notions about tryin' to take leave of us without permission. There's a hang rope waitin' fer you now out there—provided Henry Sloan don't kill you before they kin string you up. Stealin' women is a lynchin' offense in these parts."

"You gave your word that Ellen Sloan would be freed when Clem showed up," Frank said.

"But I didn't say when," Haskell said.

"How much money are you going to ask of Henry Sloan?"

Haskell pretended to calculate. "Say, fifteen thousand—no, twenty. Come to think about it I reckon twenty-five thousand would be about right fer all the trouble I've gone to."

"That's quite a sum," Frank said.

"He's good fer it—an' more," Haskell said. "He's got thousands of heads of beef scattered over a lot of range up an' down California. He's a stockholder in that bank we hit in San Berdoo, which owes us something for what happened. He owns a lot of other things. He kin raise twenty-five thousand like it was a penny ante in a poker game."

"And if he comes through, that's what it'll be," Frank said. "Just the ante. You'll maybe ask for him to sweeten the pot."

The malicious grin was on Haskell's thick lips. "Now don't go puttin' bad thoughts in my mind, Doc," he said.

"What if Henry Sloan realizes this and refuses the ante?" Frank asked.

"You do ask a lot of questions, don't you, Doc?" Haskell said harshly. "He cain't refuse. They say he's figgerin' on runnin' fer governor of the state. He would not only be through in politics, but in most everything else."

Frank had no other place to go with this conversation. He turned and began to hobble away.

"You might not know how lucky you are, Doc," Haskell called after him.

Frank paused and turned. "Lucky?"

"You better look at it sensible," Haskell said. "I sort of like yore spunk. If you can use a gun as well as you handle yore fists, you'd be a man to ride with. We could use a sawbones. You know a lot about towns an' people up an' down the line—such as folks with money, an' banks an' such that are easy to knock over if we have inside information."

"Well now," Frank said, "that's quite a surprising offer. Do you think I'd make a good murderer?"

Haskell's expression became wicked. "Don't try to act lily-white with me, Doc. I know all about you. You had a rep for bein' rough an' tough in the Army. You even got a medal. You killed your share when guerrillas tried to overrun a field hospital where you was in charge. They was human beings, even though they might not have been your color."

"I've saved the lives of a few too," Frank said. "Including some who tried to wipe us out that day. They weren't my color either. I've maybe saved some of your kind too, like that young thug there in the tent with Blackie. He's going to pull through, I'm afraid."

"Of course, of course," Haskell said, deciding to become bland and oily. "I've seen you in action, you know. I saw you handle Pete, here, a while ago. An' that camp boss and cook at Pima Flat. Think it over about joinin' us. You'll be rollin' in money in a year or two. There's Mexico, not far away. There's the Argentine where they say the señoritas are mightly comely. It'd be better'n workin' for beans an' tamales fer the railroad an' livin' in this howlin' desert."

"I'll think it over," Frank said.

"Now that's bein' sensible," Haskell said. "An' while yo're thinkin' about it, keep this here law dodger in mind. Five thousand dollars is a lot of money on yore head an' mine. I'm offerin' you the only chance you've got of livin' to a ripe old age."

The Haskells walked away, grinning. Lily came from the tent and gazed grimly at him. "We heard," she said. "Maybe he is telling you what is best for you."

"You could be right," Frank said.

Ellen Sloan spoke. "Lily said they showed you some kind of a printed paper. What was it?"

"Your father believes I'm a member of this outfit and that I set up your kidnaping," Frank said. "He's offering five thousand dollars reward for me, dead or alive."

"He can't really believe that," she exclaimed.

"It seems that Clem Haskell must have convinced him," Frank said. "And, sooner or later, he'll have other reasons for not caring whether I'm taken dead or alive."

"You mean—mean about—about—?" she choked.

"He doesn't know you are blind, as best I can determine," Frank said. "The Haskells probably are keeping that from him for fear he might decide the price they are asking is too high."

Lily Ling came at him like a tiger, beating against his chest with her small fists. "How cruel can you be?" she panted. "How brutal! Do not believe him, Ellen! He does not mean it!"

Frank caught her arms, holding her helpless. He was not watching her. His attention was concentrated on Ellen Sloan. She was standing there, stricken, as though she was the one on whom the blows were falling. Then tears, great tears of sadness began to stain her cheeks. They came from eyes that still could not see.

Again Frank had failed. He had attempted a medical trick on the soldier who had been blinded in battle in the Philippines. Shock had brought sight back to the soldier. But it had failed on Ellen Sloan. She only stood there crushed, hurt, humiliated. Then she turned and groped her way back into the tent.

"I'm afraid you are right, Doctor," she choked.

CHAPTER 10

Frank sat in the shade of the girls' tent bandaging his ankles. The shackles had rubbed the flesh nearly raw, and he was using ointment from his supplies and arranging the bandages so as to ease the endless torture.

Bart Haskell had brought the medical case and had freed the shackles for the moment, then had retreated to the mess table and was playing poker. The stakes were small at Haskell's order, palpably to hold down dissension among his lawless crew, but also because the ruffians were short of ready cash.

Hong Kong had been assigned to stand guard over the captives, and the half-caste, armed with a six-shooter and a club, which he placed within reach, lolled on the mattress under the sun shelter.

Frank's glance rested on Hong Kong's gun at intervals, always moving swiftly away before the half-caste could see the desperation in him and the longing to take possession of the weapon. Hope was finally dying, if there had ever really been any hope of escape. This was the third day of their captivity in the hide-out, and with each passing hour he felt that their chances were dwindling. Escape had become such an obsession with him that he wondered about his sanity at even thinking of trying to seize Hong Kong's gun with the card players so close at hand. Such an attempt would only bring a shoot-out against impossible odds.

The two girls still had the knife that Lily had seized from

Luke Clay, but he did not know where it was hidden, and they had refused to discuss it. He could not blame them for their silence, for that weapon was impossibly feeble in any attempt to escape from the oasis, watched as they were every moment.

At times he almost envied them. At least they had a way of escape from torture and misery. As for himself, he knew that his pretense at considering joining the outlaws had not deluded Bart Haskell.

Haskell was having other problems. Ugly unrest was growing among the desperadoes. Evidently no word had come from Henry Sloan as to meeting the cash demand for his daughter's release, at least as far as Frank knew. The heliograph had brought no word that he had seen.

Bart Haskell's mood, especially, was turning more morose and dangerous as time passed. Squabbles among the outlaws were growing more frequent. Some of these had come almost to the point of gunplay at times. Frank felt that a real explosion was in the making.

It came at the poker table over some trivial matter of whether a player had met his two-bit ante. Haskell reared up, lunged across the plank table, and grasped one of the players by the throat. His quarry was a wizened, ratlike man known as Crip because he limped on a shortened leg—shortened by a bullet in the past, Frank surmised.

Haskell dragged the smaller man across the table. His victim tried to draw his six-shooter, but the outlaw leader twisted it from his hand. Then he jammed the weapon against the man's stomach and pulled the trigger twice. The reports were heavy and muffled by the victim's body. Crip was dead when Haskell pushed him away and let him slump to the ground.

Dead, dread silence came in the camp. The powder fumes drifted about, then began to fade in the hot afternoon sun. Men were crouching, staring with the foxlike expression of animals. Some had their hands on their guns. One of these was Pete Mace. He and some of the others had likely been friendly with Crip, or, more to the point, were hoping for enough backing to challenge Haskell's action. They failed, for the odds remained against them.

Clem Haskell was the first to move. He had not been in the game, but had been lolling in a hammock in the shade of his father's tent. He came to his feet, darted a few paces to his right, his pistol in his hand. In that position he protected his father from being flanked.

For a space the silence continued to hold. Then Pete Mace let his hand drop away from his six-shooter. Once again he did not have the sand to go through with the challenge. He even forced a sick grin. His backers followed suit. Some of them turned away, plainly angered that Mace had not had the sand to go through with it. He had again lost his chance to try to take over leadership of the organization.

"Take him away an' plant him," Bart Haskell said, waving the muzzle of his pistol toward Crip's body. "You, Luke, an' Monk. Some o' the rest o' you kin lend a hand. Bury him well away from the camp an' the pond so that he don't stink up the place. I don't want no coyotes diggin' him up. He might try to ha'nt me." He forced a guffaw. "Not that I'm skeered of ghosts nor of any man alive. Crip wasn't any use to us. He's one less we'll have to split up with."

Frank finished caring for his ankles. He was sure that Lily had been watching from the tent flap and had seen the killing. The flap was now closed.

He spoke softly. "It's all over."

It was Ellen Sloan who answered. "For now, at least. Lily has told me what happened. It proves one thing. They are divided. It is only fear of that brute that keeps them from leaping at his throat. Lily said some of them were about to make an issue of it, but were afraid to go through with it."

"That's about the size of it," Frank said.

"We must try to divide them further," she said.

Frank uttered a warning for silence then, for Bart Haskell was heading in their direction, along with one of the outlaws.

"What was you talkin' about?" Haskell demanded. He was in a savage mood as the result of the killing. To emphasize the question he cuffed Frank on the head with the barrel of his six-shooter. The blow was not intended to really injure, but Frank rubbed his scalp and was relieved to find that the skin had not been broken. But it would add to his collection of bruises and scars. He hastily replaced his hat, which he had laid aside, as protection against further punishment.

"Zack Card, here, will take a turn at watchin' over you three," Haskell said. "See to it, Zack, that they don't do any more powwow."

Frank had heard of an outlaw named Zack Card, and he was now meeting the man at first hand. He was much more fastidious of garb than the other members of the gang. He was said to be a gambler as well as an outlaw, and he apparently tried to dress the part, for he was a study in black and white—black-handled six-shooter in a black holster, black wide-brimmed plantation hat, black boots and trousers, and a white shirt and black string tie. He sported a small black waxed mustache and sideburns.

"I'll take care of things, Bart," he said.

"I've been wondering why your blinker hasn't been talking today," Frank said to Haskell.

"Never mind about that," Haskell spat. "Ain't it about

time you tuk a look at Denny? An' from now on, no talkin' to these gals unless one of us is around to hear what's bein' said."

Frank started to head toward the tent where the wounded outlaws were housed, but Haskell halted him. "Jest a minute, Doc," he said. "Yo're forgettin' yore jewelry."

He picked up the shackles, produced the key, and locked the bands on Frank's bandaged ankles. Frank hobbled to the hospital tent. Blackie's pallet was vacant, for the outlaw had talked some of his pals into making improvised crutches, and had improved enough to make his way to the mess table and take part in the poker game.

It had been touch and go for hour after hour with Denny. He had drifted between life and death. But the instant Frank entered the tent he saw that he had won the fight. The fever was gone from Denny's hollow cheeks. He was definitely over the hill.

Denny knew it also. He put together the ghost of a triumphal smile. "I've made it, haven't I, Doc?" he husked. "I'm over the hill. An' I've still got my laig."

"It looks that way," Frank said. "You'll likely limp for a while, at least, but that won't keep you out of trouble, I imagine."

"I ain't goin' to be a crip like—like—" Denny began plaintively.

"Like the one Bart Haskell murdered?" Frank asked.

Denny sobered. His sunken eyes darted toward Zack Card, who had followed Frank and was standing near the flap. "Maybe Crip had it comin' to him," he stammered.

"I suppose you'll be safe enough around Bart as long as you obey orders and come to heel when he snaps his fingers," Frank said.

"I ain't nobody's heel-dog," Denny blustered, stung by

the scorn in Frank's voice. "Not Bart's anyway. I ain't afeared of him." Then, remembering the listening Zack Card, he lowered his voice. "I want to thank you, Doc, fer what you've done fer me. I'd have croaked if it hadn't been fer you an' I know it."

"Just so you don't decide to pull that gun on me again, we'll call it even," Frank said.

What he wanted was for Denny to make some move that might give him a clue as to the location of the hidden weapon. But he failed.

Zack Card spoke. "Come out of there, Doc. I heard you soft-soapin' Denny about Crip. Denny, you danged fool, all the doc wants is to git us fightin' among ourselves so that it might give him a chance at whatever he's got in mind."

"Now, why would I have anything in mind now that the law wants me along with the rest of you," Frank said. "And it seems that I'm worth more than the most of you, dead or alive."

He returned to his pallet. He had again started to build up desperate plans if he could get possession of a gun—Denny's gun—any gun. But it continued to be only a lost hope, along with all the other schemes he had tried to formulate. Ellen Sloan's belief that a split might be brought among the outlaws apparently was vain also, for Zack Card had revealed that he was aware of it, and that meant Haskell was also aware.

Lily came hurrying from the nursery tent. "It is the baby!" she said breathlessly. "I cannot awaken him! The mother has given permission for you to come—if you will."

Frank hobbled to the tent. Mary Wong lay with the sheet modestly pulled over her face. The tiny boy lay in a crib that Lily had improvised from a packing box. She had found soft coverlets somewhere.

The child lay limp and did not respond when Frank tried

to awaken him. He sent Zack Card to fetch the medical kit. When it was brought he saw that it contained only his stethoscope and thermometer. Bart Haskell was taking no chances. He had removed the scalpels, surgical saw, and probe. Also the few drugs that had remained.

The baby was apparently in a very deep sleep, limp and drained of strength. It only whimpered faintly now and then. Lily had contrived a cloth over the mouth of a whiskey bottle to serve for nursing. The bottle contained what looked like milk.

"It is condensed milk," Lily explained. "There are many cases of it in camp. I add sugar and water to it. She can no longer nurse him herself."

Frank became aware of a foreign, sweetish odor. He examined the nursing bottle more closely, sniffing. Mary Wong pulled the sheet from her eyes so that she could watch apprehensively. Her face, what he could see of it, was marked by hard life that was aging her prematurely, although he judged that she was no more than in her late twenties. However, contrarily, her eyes held a mother's fear for her child.

He squeezed some of the liquid into his palm and tasted it. He looked accusingly at Mary Wong.

"No wonder he sleeps too much," he said. "Opium."

"Opium?" Lily gasped. "Oh no!"

Mary Wong did not deny it. "Only a leetle," she said. "I put it in when you were not here. Only a very leetle. I *had* to make him sleep."

Frank left the tent, emptied the bottle into the soil. "Wash it out and make a new batch of milk," he told Lily. "The baby needs to wake up and do some howling and kicking. Then we'll see how much damage has been done. He's doped now. Lucky he isn't dead. He seems to come from tough stock."

"The terrible one told me he will take the baby away if it disturbs his sleep again," Mary Wong moaned. "That is why I do it."

"Where did you get the opium?" Frank asked.

She gave him a bitter, tired smile and looked around. Frank saw two opium pipes in the tent. "It is the forgetfulness of my people from the hardships in this land where we are not wanted," she said. She looked at the infant, whom Lily was holding in her arms. "Why do I want him to live?" she went on. "He would be much happier if he joined his ancestors in the heavenly gardens. He will know only misery and want on this earth."

Frank had no answer for that. It was obvious, because of her use of English, that, like Lily, this outlaw's woman had been born and educated in America. He discovered that Ellen Sloan had joined them, with Zack Card close at hand. She had found her way alone across the camp site to the nursery tent. Blindness already was apparently sharpening her perceptions. Frank had insisted that she continue to protect her eyes with a damp, cool bandage, and she was still faithfully following that instruction.

"Bring water and bathe the baby," he told Lily. "Keep him as cool and comfortable as possible. He will be feverish and crying when he awakens. Try to make him nurse from the bottle. If there's talcum and baby ointment in camp, have Haskell find it. They've stolen about everything else, maybe they've got something useful for babies."

He spoke to Mary Wong. "You must not want your son to die. It is not for you to decide such a thing."

Mary Wong again hid her face from him. "It is not a thing I want to talk about," she said in a muffled voice. "I am ashamed, but I thought it was best for him."

"No more opium," Frank warned. "It is bad, very bad,

for anyone, let alone so young a baby, no matter how little you have used. No more, do you understand?"

On an impulse he placed the baby in Ellen Sloan's arms. She was startled, confused. Then he could see that she was pleased. "He is very small, isn't he?" she said.

After a time, with the baby already beginning to show evidence of drifting into a more restless, but more normal pattern, Frank left the tent along with Lily and Ellen Sloan. "Get your hands on that opium," he breathed in Lily's ear, so that Zack Card could not hear.

"Why do you want it, Doctah?" she murmured.

But Frank did not dare answer, for Card had moved closer to listen suspiciously.

A new commotion was rising among the outlaws at the mess table. The card game had halted. Men were on their feet staring up at the ridge.

The heliograph was blinking. Bart Haskell left the table, shouldering men aside, and strode into the open where he could have a clear view. The blinker kept flashing.

"What's Whitey sayin', Bart?" one of the group demanded.

Haskell did not answer. He stood there until the blinker had gone lifeless. He continued to delay speaking as though hoping for additional information. There was something in his expression that puzzled Frank. It was a mixture of cunning and speculation. He realized the man was not actually expecting more news. He was thinking. He seemed to be rolling over in his mind a thought that was both attractive and dangerous.

Haskell reached a decision. He turned to the waiting outlaws and made a disgusted gesture. "Nothin'," he said. "Whitey jest said he was gittin' sick an' tired of settin' up there all day, lookin' at sand dunes. Nothin' in sight, an' no word from old Moneybags. Whitey will be down as soon as he gets the word there'll be nothing more for the night."

The outlaws, disappointed, subsided with grunts and oaths of anger. "So what about it, Bart?" Pete Mace demanded, making one more try to regain some of the face he had lost. "Are we goin' to set here twiddlin' our fingers while Henry Sloan makes up his mind? He's been given plenty o' time. It looks like he maybe don't think his daughter is worth twenty-five thousand dollars." Mace turned and glared balefully toward the tent that housed the hostages. "We want to know just what yo're goin' to do about it, Bart," he continued.

"Looks like old Moneybags needs a little proddin'," Haskell said. "Maybe he wants proof that we've really got his daughter, or that she's still alive."

"Such as maybe that lady finger Clem talked about?" Mace asked, his viciousness coming completely to the surface. "I mean a real lady finger like the doc here could saw off, neat an' purty?"

"I don't reckon we need to go that far yet," Haskell said. "A thing like that might come in handy later. Clem an' me will ride out tonight to see Steve an' send some messages to Henry Sloan that will get some action."

"How about me goin' with you?" Mace demanded.

"Clem an' me will take care of it," Haskell snapped, and walked away.

Mace, scowling, dissatisfied, rejoined his companions who settled down, still grumbling, but resigning themselves to more waiting.

Frank had not been able to read every word of the message that had been flashed from the ridge, but he was sure he had interpreted the gist of it:

TERMS AGREED. MONEY WILL BE AT PLACE NAMED.
MUST HAVE PROOF DAUGHTER IS STILL ALIVE.

Haskell beckoned his son, and they retreated into the tent they occupied. Frank found a place where he could keep an eye on that tent. He was sure Bart was taking his son into his confidence. He was also sure that a double cross was in the making. Bart Haskell had lied to his men as to the real purport of the message.

As dusk approached, Whitey, the lookout, rode into camp on a saddle mule, his lonely vigil on the ridge over for the day. Bart Haskell strode to intercept him, and stood, a hand on the neck of Whitey's horse, talking fast for a time. Frank watched Whitey's reaction. The man seemed a little startled at first, but continued to listen intently as Bart kept talking. Haskell brought a drink for Whitey from the whiskey keg, which Whitey downed. He nodded, with a tight smile, as he handed the tin cup back. Haskell slapped him on the knee, and Whitey rode on away through camp to put up his horse in the flat.

Frank was sure a pact had been made. Whitey, knowing the real wording of the message, had been taken into whatever scheme Haskell had in mind. That was by necessity. The plan, Frank guessed, was to delude the rank and file of the outlaw organization while the Haskells made off with the ransom that Henry Sloan evidently had placed at some point that Haskell had indicated.

A bony, loose-jointed outlaw with long thin arms was given the next stretch as guard over the captives. He was known as Monk among his companions because of his physical appearance. He had served as guard on previous occasions, and Lily was deathly afraid of him. Like the others, Monk had no liking for the task, and settled down, grumbling and blaming the captives, hoping for some excuse to vent his anger on them.

The Chinese baby was beginning to respond to the simple treatment Frank had prescribed. When it cried for food, its voice was growing so lusty its mother was beginning to be terrified that it would annoy Bart Haskell to the point of carrying out his threat to take the child from her.

Frank waited until Lily returned from one of her visits to the nursery tent, then sent Monk to bring his medical kit on the excuse that he needed it to see that Denny was making out for the night.

"The opium?" he whispered as soon as Monk was out of earshot. "Did you find it?"

"Not yet," Lily answered. "It must be in a wooden chest that she keeps back of her bed. That seems to be where she had all that she values. I do not know how I can look into it without arousing her suspicion. You have a use for it? A plan?"

"I'm not sure," he admitted. "It's a long shot. Haskell is hoodwinking the others. He aims to keep all the ransom himself."

"The ransom? It has been paid?"

"From what I could read on the blinker, Haskell lied when he told the others there was no news. The money is waiting at some place that he evidently designated, but her father seems to want proof that Miss Sloan is still alive."

"Proof?" Lily echoed. "What is this proof he wants?"

It was Ellen Sloan who answered. "One of my fingers, perhaps, as Clem said."

"Don't be ridiculous!" Frank snapped. "Clem was only trying to scare you. It looks like Haskell doesn't intend to divide up any money he squeezes out of Henry Sloan. Because nobody else in the gang is able to read the blinker, he might get away with it. He's had to take Whitey in on it, of course, and probably the man who forwards the messages from down on the desert. I've heard them name him as Steve. I doubt if either Whitey or Steve will live long enough to enjoy any share Haskell has promised them."

"When will Haskell get the money?" Ellen Sloan asked.

"He and his son are riding out tonight. The others think he intends to try to shake up your father into paying the ransom. In reality I'm sure he intends to pick up the money."

"And ride away with it?" she asked.

There was no point in evading, for Frank was sure Ellen Sloan's mind was traveling along the same path as his own. "They might," he said. "They might figure a bird in hand is worth a whole flock in the sky."

"What you're saying is that you believe the Haskells will come back here and try to squeeze my father out of more money in return for my—my release. Or my life."

"Yes," Frank said grimly.

There was silence between them for a space. Lily spoke. "I will try again to find the opium, Doctah."

"Do you know what you are risking?" Frank asked.

She answered with Oriental fatalism. "I am not what these man call the goose that lays the golden eggs, whatever that means. When there is nothing to lose, there is nothing to risk."

Frank again felt the coldness inside him. It was as though the Chinese girl had written off her life as lost. "It has been very good to know you, Lily," he said.

"If I do not find the opium, it will be bad for us," she said. "Is it our only hope?"

"Of course not," Frank said, trying to sound scoffing, and failing. "Luck comes and goes. So far we've had none that was good, but it might turn our way. These cursed shackles are a big factor against us. Haskell has the key, but getting it is the problem, and my guess is that he will take it with him when he rides out tonight. Denny has a six-gun hidden somewhere around his bed. I haven't found just where, and, to tell the truth, I don't really know what

I'd do with it. One gun against a dozen men isn't likely to get us far."

"Prayers will do it," she said firmly.

"Prayers and a pinch or two of opium," Frank said. "I'm sure your prayers will be heard."

"And Ellen's also. I pray in my faith, and she prays in her religion. She prays for her fathah. And she prays for you, Doctah."

"Please, Lily!" Ellen Sloan, who had been listening, burst out.

"It is time it is said," Lily went on. "She prays that she will be able to reach her fathah before you and he meet. She fears for her fathah. She fears his pride, his bitterness toward doctahs. And now he has been told that you are a member of this gang of brutes, and that you were a party to having her kidnaped."

Monk, returning, must have heard the whispering, and came hurrying. "That's enough gab," he snarled. "What was you hatchin' up, Doc?"

"How to get my share of the money that Bart is trying to collect from Henry Sloan," Frank answered.

Monk uttered a guffaw. "Yore share? What'n blazes put any notion in yore head that you've got any share comin'?"

"I've got the name, I ought to have the game," Frank said. "I'm in as deep as you, maybe deeper. There's five thousand dollars on my scalp. I'm branded as one of this outfit. The way I see it, I've got no choice. I'm entitled to my cut of any money Bart wrings out of Henry Sloan."

"I've got a picture of the boys standin' for handin' any money over to you," Monk sneered. "It's goin' to be sliced thin enough as it is, with all these jiggers here in camp, not to mention quite a few on the outside that are helpin' us."

"How about my kit?" Frank asked.

"Bart didn't have time to bother," Monk said. "He's busy gittin' ready to—"

Monk broke off, for the two Haskells had emerged from their tent and were striding purposefully toward them. Clem Haskell carried a lighted lantern, and his father was brandishing a wicked-looking sheath knife.

CHAPTER 11

"You there, the Sloan gal!" Bart Haskell snapped. "Come out here!"

Frank heard Ellen Sloan utter a sharp sigh of fear. She did not appear. Haskell burst into the tent, followed by his son. From the sounds they apparently had seized Ellen Sloan, and she was struggling. Lily Ling uttered a cry of anger and Frank heard the report of a palm on flesh. Then a heavier blow. The Chinese girl moaned in pain and reeled against the wall of the tent so close to Frank that he braced her from falling with the thickness of the canvas between them.

"You chink hellcat!" Haskell raged. "Stay out of this!"

"You awful cowards!" Lily screamed. "She cannot see to defend herself. What are you going to do with that knife?"

"I ain't hurtin' her—at least right now," Haskell snorted. "All I want is a bunch of her hair an' that gold locket she's wearin'. Stand still, gal. It'll be yore fault if the knife slips. All I want is to make sure that Moneybags knows we've got you an' that we mean business."

"Very well," Ellen Sloan spoke. In contrast to Lily she seemed calm. "Take the locket, but there is a picture in it that means nothing to you but much to me. It could be of no value to you."

"A picture?" Haskell said. Evidently he had opened the locket. "It's of a lady. Say, she looks like you."

"My mother," Ellen Sloan said. "She is dead."

That silenced Haskell for a moment. "All right!" he finally blurted out. "Keep the picture, but I take the locket, an' a lock o' that purty hair. What good will a picture do you when you can't see it?"

"What a cruel thing to say," Lily Ling burst out. "What kind of a man are you?"

Haskell's reply was another blow. Frank hobbled to stand just outside the flap of the tent. He was there when the Haskells emerged. Bart held in one hand a thick lock of Ellen Sloan's coppery hair, along with the gold locket. The thin gold chain, broken again, dangled from his fingers.

"What you doin' here?" the outlaw leader demanded, still in a rage over Lily's words and her opposition. "Git back on yore blanket!" He still had the knife in his hand and was in a mood to murder. But his son intervened.

"Not now, Bart," Clem said. "We might need a sawbones ag'in."

The elder Haskell roughly pushed Frank aside and headed away. "As Clem says, we might have work fer you, fella," he said. "Maybe a lock of hair won't convince ol' Moneybags. We might have to send him somethin' more personal. Such as an ear or a finger—a lady finger."

He began shouting orders that horses and pack animals be brought up from the remuda, and water bags filled. "I want to make a fast trip an' be back some time tomorrow," he told the outlaws. "Clem an' me kin make it to Steve's place before midnight an' have him send a message that'll put a burr under Moneybags' tail to let him understand we don't aim to let him stall around any longer if he wants to see his daughter alive ag'in."

Frank spoke to Lily Ling. "Are you hurt?"

"No," she said, but her voice was shaking.

"I want to take a look at you," Frank said. "Light the lantern. I'm coming in."

Monk started to object. "Now, I don't reckon I ought to let you—"

Frank did not heed, but entered the tent and lowered the flap in Monk's face. He took the match from Lily's shaking hand and lighted the lantern. Ellen Sloan's hair hung below her shoulder, and there was a gap where Haskell had knifed away a length. A bruise showed where the locket had been torn from her throat.

Blood seeped from a corner of the Chinese girl's mouth, but the injury was superficial. Frank sent Monk to bring water in a basin and a clean towel.

"Forget about the opium," he said. "It's too dangerous for you."

"No," she said. "I will try to get it tonight."

Ellen Sloan spoke. "If I could only change places with you, Lily. I am such a burden." She was drooping, the strength and spirit suddenly crushed out of her. "It just isn't fair," she sobbed.

Monk arrived with water and towels. Frank treated Lily's injury, then arranged another damp compress and adjusted it over Ellen Sloan's eyes. "It's all I can do right now," he said. "I wish I could do more."

Monk was standing in the flap. "Come out'n there, Doc," he said. "Come out before Bart finds out I'm letting you talk to the gals. He ain't in the best of happiness, for he's in fer a long ride."

Frank obeyed, hobbling slowly back to his pallet, making sure his chains clanked dismally. Sounds, faint at that distance, indicated that animals were being saddled. He had learned that the horses and pack mules were always rounded up before dark and evidently held in some enclosure where they would be more easily available and safer from possible attack by wolves or cougars.

Full darkness had come by the time two saddled horses

were brought into camp, along with a pair of sinewy pack mules which were loaded with water bags.

"We'll be back late tomorrow, most likely," Bart said as he and his son mounted. "Jem, you'll be in charge. The rest of you do what Jem Blair tells you, or you'll have me to answer to. I'm warnin' you."

The Haskells rode out of camp into the darkness, with Frank straining his eyes, hoping to solve the secret of the right path to follow to find the way out of the oasis. Darkness foiled him.

The outlaws had eaten and were settling down to their nightly poker game. Visits to the whiskey keg became more frequent. Jem Blair, the outlaw Haskell had named to take charge, was doing his share of the imbibing. He was a paunchy, tobacco-chewing ruffian, foul-mouthed and watery-eyed. It became apparent that the others had little respect for him. His appointment, of course, had been another deliberate slap at Pete Mace's ambition to lead the organization. Mace was sitting apart from the others, obviously smoldering with resentment. It was evident he had some support.

Frank began racking his brain, seeking some plan that might serve to widen the rift between the factions. He knew that even if he succeeded, the matter would likely end in a gun fight that might involve not only himself but the two girls. Like all his other plans, he believed this was too great a chance to take.

The feeble wailing of the baby arose in the distance. Frank heard Lily pull on her sandals. She emerged from the tent, gave him a little determined gesture, and hurried to respond to the mother who was shouting for her. He knew that she intended to try again to locate the opium.

Lantern light glowed in the nursery tent, and shadows moved gigantically on the canvas wall. Monk left his post and visited the whiskey keg. He lingered at the mess table to watch the poker game, helping himself to libations from the tin cup in his hand. With the Haskells gone, discipline was relaxed.

Lily returned and entered the tent. She did not speak for a time, and when she did so Frank was forced to press his ear close to the canvas wall to hear, for she was sobbing with despair. "I am sorry," she wept. "There is no more opium. Mary Wong has destroyed it so that she would not be tempted to use it again on the little baby. She told me that she did it because she knows you told the truth when you said it was the wrong thing to do."

Frank was silent. One more possible avenue of escape was closed. Perhaps the last one.

"There might be another way," Lily said. "There is this, what you call it, chloral something or other."

"Chloral hydrate," Frank said slowly. "When did you learn about that?"

"I was there when you were first treating the two men who had been shot," she explained. "Would it not do the same as the opium?"

"Even more so," Frank said. "The only trouble is that I don't know where it is. Haskell knows what knockout drops can do. He took it and what few other drugs I had from my kit along with anything else that I might use as a weapon."

"Would it be hidden in their tent?" she asked.

"Maybe," Frank said. "But it might as well be in Timbuktu. With these shackles clanking I wouldn't have a chance of getting into that tent to look for it, drunk as they'll likely be before long."

"I wear no chains," the Chinese girl said.

Ellen Sloan had been listening. "No," she spoke. "No, dear Lily. It is too dangerous. If they caught you . . ." She left it unfinished.

"What is your plan, Doctah, if I could find this thing whose name I can't remember?" Lily said calmly.

"The same as with the opium," Frank said. "Try to slip a pinch or so into the guard's whiskey. Then try to get to the horses."

"It was in a brown bottle, was it not?" Lily murmured.

"Yes, but you heard what Miss Sloan said."

"I heard," the Chinese girl answered.

"Don't try it," Frank said. "We'll think of something else."

She did not answer. After a time he decided that she had agreed with him. The revelry at the mess table was growing. The bickering increased in proportion to the drinking. The outlaws built a roaring bonfire for light. Its glow reached over the camp.

Luke Clay came to stand guard over the captives. He had been drinking and was savagely quarrelsome. His first effort was to prod Frank roughly in the ribs with the toe of his boot. "Just give me an excuse to really work on you, fella," he growled.

Frank decided against giving him such an opening and remained silent. "Yalla, huh?" Clay sneered. He had brought whiskey in a tin cup, which he drained. After a time he again headed for the mess table, but in reality for the whiskey keg to refill his cup.

The faint sound of canvas being slit came from the nearby tent. Frank realized what was happening. An opening was being cut in the rear wall of the tent—with the knife that had been taken from Luke Clay, no doubt.

"Wait!" he exclaimed. "No, Lily. It's too dangerous."

There was no answer. Presently Ellen Sloan spoke. "She is gone. She is trying it."

Frank moved to a better view of the camp. The glow of the bonfire lighted a wide area, and he crouched, staring tensely, knowing how much more dangerous this made the attempt by the Chinese girl.

He scanned the far shadows, trying to catch sight of her. Luke Clay still lingered at the mess table, a tin cup in his hand. Finally he succeeded. It was a mere glimpse as she faded into the tent that the Haskells used. She had made it that far at least, and now the bonfire was an ally, for its light would penetrate the walls of the tent enough to help her in the search.

Time passed. Luke Clay came back to his post, bringing his tin cup. He was muttering and Frank expected more trouble. But Clay, evidently believing the captives were asleep, decided to return to the more interesting mess table.

Many more minutes passed. Then Frank glimpsed Lily again, fading off into the shadows beyond the Haskell tent. He tensed, hoping against hope there would be no shout of discovery. None came, but Luke Clay was now heading back to his post. But he heard faint sounds inside the tent against whose walls he was pressing his ear.

Lily spoke in a murmur. "I have the brown bottle, Doctah."

"Thank God," Frank said.

"How will I get this thing into his cup?" she asked.

Frank shrank again from the decision, but it had gone this far with luck running their way. "I'll kick up a commotion to bring him to me," he said hurriedly. "If the sign is right, maybe you can sneak out and drop some in his cup. He always brings whiskey back with him."

"How much will I use?"

"A pinch of it. A big pinch."

"Will he die?"

"Not that kind. I'm only hoping it will knock him out long enough for—"

He quit talking, for Luke Clay was near at hand. The

man was well into his cups, and evidently in a more jovial mood, for he made no attempt to approach Frank. He set his tin cup of whiskey carefully on a flat rock alongside the mattress and stretched out. He pulled out a silver pocket watch and held it to the moon, evidently to ascertain how much longer he would be obliged to remain on guard before summoning a new sentinel.

Frank pretended that he was asleep, breathing steadily. He heard the girls follow his example. Clay grunted and helped himself to another sip from the tin cup. The moon floated back of a higher ridge, and the oasis was dark and ghostly, for the bonfire was beginning to fade to dull crimson embers.

Frank suddenly uttered a yelp and began thrashing around. He staggered to his feet, kicking and clanking the chain.

Luke Clay, who had been half asleep, reared to his feet, his six-shooter in his hand. "What's wrong with you?" he exploded. "You havin' a fit?"

"It's a snake!" Frank panted. "A sidewinder! I felt it crawl across my leg. My God, man! Be careful! A bite from a sidewinder can kill you in minutes."

Clay hastily backed to safer distance, peering around. "Whar did it go?" he croaked.

"There it is!" Frank said, pointing to the rear corner of the tent. "Kill it! Shoot it!"

Luke Clay, in mortal fear of the deadly small rattlesnake of the desert, moved in that direction, his gun ready. "Whar? Whar?" he croaked. "I don't see it!"

He continued to circle to the rear of the tent, keeping carefully clear of any shadow that might offer cover for the serpent that was not there.

From the corner of an eye Frank saw Lily—again a

mere shadow—scuttle from the tent to where Clay's tin cup sat. She scuttled back into the tent.

Luke Clay moved cautiously around the tent. Frank feared the man would see the slit in the rear wall, but the outlaw's attention was fixed on avoiding possible danger at his feet, and he circled back to Frank's side. "I don't see no snake," he said. "You sure you wasn't dreamin'? If there was one he's gone now."

Clay returned to his post and emptied the tin cup to settle his nerves. He continued to keep peering around, still uneasy. He mumbled for a time. He finally evidently decided he needed more stimulant, for he headed toward the mess table. He didn't make it. He began to sway. His knees buckled, and he settled face down on the ground, breathing wheezily.

The revelry at the mess table had taken its toll, now that discipline was relaxed. Only two outlaws remained at the table and they were talking maudlinly. The others had staggered off to bed.

"Wait!" Frank whispered. He tensely watched the two survivors. One of them finally pillowed his head on his arms on the mess table and succumbed to the liquor. The other staggered off to bed in one of the huts. The camp was deserted, lighted only by the crimson glow of the dying bonfire.

"All right!" Frank said. The girls came from the tent, fully dressed. Lily, leading her companion, looked to Frank for instructions. He first took Clay's six-shooter and gun belt and buckled it on. There were half a dozen extra shells in the belt loops.

"I've got to do something about these," he said, indicating the shackles. "Then we'll try to get horses."

He first ripped strips from a sheet on one of the cots and

used them as pads around the chain and shackles to muffle sound. "To the blacksmith shop," he breathed.

Hobbling along between the two girls, his arms over their shoulders, gave him greater mobility. Lily kept looking toward the huts and to where Luke Clay lay sprawled. But no sign of awakening came.

The blacksmith forge fire was cold, with tools lying around. Frank upset the anvil with a surge of his shoulder. He sat down, spreading his legs so that the chain was stretched on a corner of the metal weight. He motioned Lily to hand him a mallet which he swung.

Once, twice, and again. The pads of cloth muffled the impact somewhat, but the sounds seemed fearfully loud to him. He swung again, with desperate strength. A smashed link in the chain parted. He still had the clamps around his ankles, with short sections of chain dangling, but, at least, he was no longer hobbled.

Lily uttered a warning sound. In the pale of the dying bonfire Frank saw that one of the outlaws had appeared from a hut.

The moon was emerging from behind the peak and its light was moving across the oasis toward them.

"Down!" Frank husked. He drew Ellen Sloan flat on the ground beside him. Lily also lay prone, and both girls edged close to him in an instinctive need for protection.

The lone figure in the distant camp seemed to be peering around uncertainly, evidently trying to locate the source of whatever had awakened him. He wore only his underdrawers, and he was very unsteady on his feet, evidently still drunk.

He finally wandered to the whiskey keg, helped himself to potent drink, then staggered back into the tent from which he had come.

Frank forced a wait of more minutes to make sure the man would not emerge again. "Now!" he finally breathed. "No noise! But move as fast as possible."

All he knew about the livestock was that the animals were corralled at night somewhere beyond the flat. He lifted Ellen Sloan in his arms, carrying her for the sake of speed.

He heard the stir and snuffling and scuffling of animals ahead. He was still carrying Ellen Sloan in his arms when he tripped over a small obstruction. He managed to twist and take the force of the headlong fall with his own body, but he was stunned for a few seconds.

He forced himself to shake off the shock, and arose, gasping. "Are you hurt?" he panted.

"No," Ellen Sloan said. "But leave me." He lifted her to her feet. "Oh, please leave me," she implored. "Save yourselves!"

Neither he nor Lily answered. They grasped her arms and ran ahead, speeding her along between them. The sound of milling horses became more distinct and very near. Frank made out the spidery outline of a rude barrier ahead. As he had guessed, the rumuda was being held in what evidently was a small draw. The mouth of the draw was closed with a makeshift fence and a gate of peeled poles. Saddles, headstalls, and catch ropes were stored on rocks and brush nearby.

Someone began shouting hoarsely from the distant camp. Their escape had been discovered.

The confusion in the corral was increasing. Horses began whinnying and rearing. Frank realized the danger. "Stop!" he exclaimed. "We're spooking them! Stand still!"

But he spoke too late. The animals were terrified by the appearance of running shadows in the moonlight, shadows that brought with them the scent of fear and desperation. The stampede erupted like a bursting dam.

"Run!" Frank shouted. "That gate might not hold!"

He was right. The rude barrier was no match for what struck it a moment later. Frank and Lily, literally carrying Ellen between them, managed to race clear and into the shelter of boulders and brush before the avalanche of frightened horses and mules burst free and thundered past.

The stampede roared away into the broken moonlight. The tumult faded and died in the distance, but the shouting increased at the camp as the outlaws were awakened.

"They've stole saddle mounts an' stampeded the rest o' the stock," a shrill voice came from the camp. "They've left us afoot!"

Frank and his companions were also afoot, although the outlaws seemed to believe they had had time to saddle animals and be on their way.

Frank stood for a space weighing the odds. They were surrounded by the labyrinth of ridges, rocky draws, and the ocean of dunes that composed the Devil's Playground, and there apparently was only one route out of the oasis, a route he did not know exactly how to find.

However, the shouting in the distance offered no choice. To give up this chance of escape, thin as it was, meant return to the shackles, to never again have a chance for freedom, for they would be guarded more closely in the future.

CHAPTER 12

Ellen Sloan seemed to be reading his thoughts. "You and Lily must try it," she said. "I will stay. I am the only one they really want."

"No!" Lily said. Frank did not bother to answer.

They began running. He led the way, guiding the blinded girl, trying to pick out the best route through the rocks and thorned brush.

The shouting came nearer. Loose horses, drifting aimlessly, loomed up around them at times, but the animals galloped away into the shadows when Frank tried to approach them in the hope of finding mounts.

"I cannot run any more!" Lily choked.

Frank halted and huddled down, arms around the two girls, using the deeper shadow of a boulder for protection. That eased their strained lungs. But the shouting came so close that Frank felt that discovery was certain.

He spoke to Lily. "Give me the knife."

It was Ellen who answered. "I am the one who has it. We will keep it."

"It is as we said," Lily spoke. "It is for the both of us."

Frank balanced in his hand the six-shooter he had taken from Luke Clay. Searchers were around them, calling to each other, stumbling through the brush and treacherous terrain.

"We'll never ketch any of them damned horses till it comes daylight an' we kin see to throw a rope," one of the men raged. "Whar's Jem? He's supposed to be in charge. It's up to him to figger out what to do."

If Jem Blair was within hearing, he did not respond. None of the others would accept any responsibility for the escape of the captives, especially Pete Mace, whose only words were profane criticism of Jem Blair and of Bart Haskell for putting Blair in charge of the camp.

Frank drew the girls closer against him as footsteps ground the soil nearby. He even glimpsed the silhouette of a man against the sky. Then the searcher moved onward.

For a time the outlaws continued to aimlessly try to round up mounts in the shadows, but without success. "I tell you it's no use," one snarled. "I'm goin' back to camp. I danged near busted my laig on a rock just now, kitin' around in this shambles. Them three are fur away by this time anyway, an' no tellin' which way they went."

"What do you mean, which way they went?" another growled. "There's only one way out o' this trap an' they likely found it an' are on their way. They've got horses an' they'll be out of reach come daybreak."

Frank forced patience on himself and the girls until he was sure there were no searchers around. "All right," he finally murmured. "Hand in hand. Don't ever let go."

They arose with Frank leading, followed by Ellen Sloan, who clung to his hand, and Lily bringing up the rear. They avoided the pools of moonlight. Their route was guarded by clumps of cactus and the unyielding creosote brush, and studded with boulders. The ridges above formed a jagged pattern against a sky of stars that were pale in the moonlight. Frank identified a higher ridge as the one where Whitey and his heliograph were stationed.

"We're heading in the wrong direction," he said. "There's only one way out of this place and that's at the other end of camp. We've got to sneak past the camp. Otherwise it would mean trying to climb these slants. We'd likely be lost."

Lily spoke. "When we become too much of a burden to you, Doctah, we want you to do what is sensible."

"And you would do the sensible thing also," Frank said. "By staying with a girl who is blind, and who needs you while I try to save my own hide."

"There is no sense in either of you," Ellen began. "I—"

"No talk," Frank warned. "They might hear us."

Leading them, he moved ahead again. The campfire had burned down to a wind-fanned crimson eye in the darkness well to their left. Some of the outlaws moved there, having returned to camp, and were visiting the whiskey keg. Except for the campfire there was no guiding mark, for the high ridge had merged with the outline of other summits as they progressed.

Frank lifted Ellen in his arms at times in the rough going. He was also blind now. He had no idea as to how to find the way out of the oasis. An outthrusting high ledge forced them to swing perilously close to the fringe of the outlaw camp.

Frank suddenly gripped the arms of the girls, halting them in a silent warning of danger. He could hear the shuffling sounds of someone approaching and tensed, preparing to use the muzzle of the six-shooter as a club.

He made out the approaching figure. The man halted and spoke in a husky whisper. "Is that you, Doc?"

The speaker was Denny, the wounded outlaw. He seemed to be braced on improvised canes.

"Don't move or make a noise, Denny," Frank warned. "I'm armed and will use it."

"Keep followin' the fringe of these rocks," Denny said. "You'll find the horse trail a hundred yards or so ahead, if you keep bearin' along the rocks an' circle past a big boulder. I've been waitin' fer you to come along, jest in case you needed a leetle help."

"If this is a trap, Denny . . ." Frank said.

"Nope," Denny replied. "It's a life fer a laig. A laig fer a life. It's the only way I can pay you. It's all I kin do, but yo're a long way from bein' in the clear. I reckon the desert will git you anyway."

"Has anybody gone ahead to guard the way out?" Frank asked.

"Not as fur as I know," Denny said. "They're all too drunk to think straight. An' they believe you saddled up an' headed away after stampedin' the stock. You can't miss the trail. It's easier to find yore way out than into this place. Adiós."

He turned and hobbled away, fading off into the moonlight in the direction of the camp.

"Bread cast upon the waters," Ellen sobbed.

From far away came the faint, whimpering cry of a hungry baby. Lily stood gazing back. Frank grasped her arm, heading her in the opposite direction. "No," he said.

"He is so tiny," she sighed.

"Mary Wong can take care of her own," he said. "Don't try to take all the troubles of the world on your shoulders."

They moved cautiously ahead, for they were in deep shadow, impeded by broken rock and boulders. Suddenly Frank found underfoot a trail beaten deeper than the surrounding terrain by the roofs of many animals. Denny's directions had been accurate.

They hurried along the easier going, forced to move single file. The horse trail soon led them into the black void that was the knifelike slit in the high cliff that was the secret to the oasis' immunity from discovery.

However, now that they were on foot, instead of on

horseback as they had been when they had come over this trail as captives, they found the underfooting rough and treacherous. Eventually it began to rise steadily upward, proving that the oasis they were leaving was a natural sink among the desolation. They labored over steep pitches at times. The sirocco sprang up, moaning above the narrow band of moonlight.

"Dear God, have mercy on us," Ellen spoke.

The sand deepened beneath their feet, slowing them, sapping their strength. Frank placed an arm around Ellen to help her battle the clinging sand. She would not have it.

"I will make it on my own or not at all," she said.

They plodded on. The narrow defile was behind them. The crest that had seemed so unattainable was suddenly reached. Frank and Lily halted, gazing. Ahead, beneath the yellowish moon, lay a fearsome vista—the real Playground. Great sand dunes ended the blackness through which they had been traveling, and rolled in giant combers that were white and frozen and almost luminous in the eerie light.

From far, far away came a faint, mechanical sound—the wail of a locomotive whistle. Then it was gone, brought over the miles by the whim of the wind.

"The answer to our prayers, Ellen," Lily said. "It is there. The railroad."

Here the wind had its way with them, opposing them, driving stinging sand against them, molding into new grotesque shapes the crests of the dunes, giving motion to the once-frozen sea. They could now make out the hoofprints of the horses and pack mules that had passed this way recently, but the tracks were now fading and would soon be wiped out entirely by the wind. This was the trail left by the Haskells and their animals on the way out of the Playground.

Frank gazed at the stars, located Polaris, and pointed it out to Lily. "We must keep it at our backs," he said. "The railroad is south of us."

"How far?" she asked.

"Too far," he admitted. "We will do what we can until toward daybreak. Then it'll be best to hole up and tough it out through the heat of the day, so we can travel again at night. We'll reach the railroad tomorrow night."

Ellen spoke. "Do not treat us as children, Doctor. Not after all we have been through together. Those scoundrels back there will find horses at daybreak and overtake us."

"First they've got to find us," Frank said. "We can thank the Devil for one thing. His wind covers the trails of the just as well as the unjust. This is a very big country. Three people might be just grains of sand hiding among the billions by daybreak. And a lot of them, at least, won't be too anxious to stumble across us. They know now that we're no longer helpless and that we've got fangs."

They knew that he meant the six-shooter he was carrying. "What about those two who are somewhere out there to the south?" Ellen asked. "The Haskells?"

"What about them?"

"They are on their way to get the money my father is supposed to pay for my release," she said.

Frank did not answer for a space, for he was thinking of the word she had used, "supposed."

She again seemed to pick his mind. "The money may not have been there," she said slowly.

"Of course it would be," Frank snapped. "What put a thought like that in your mind?"

"I know my father," she said, her voice level.

"Your fathah loves you, Ellen dear," Lily burst out. "Why, he almost went out of his mind when he thought you might die. He threatened to kill Dr. Conroy."

"I know," Ellen said. "He would have done it too, I'm afraid. In a way he probably thought that would make up for everything."

"For everything?" Frank asked slowly.

"When I was born my father resented the fact I was a girl," she said. "He took it as a reflection on his manhood. He already had one son to carry on his name. He avoided me when I was a baby, ignored me as a child. Oh, I didn't want for material things. Dresses, parties. He sent me to the best schools. He never came to my parties, never pretended that I was anything more than a useless part of the family —until my brother died, along with my mother. He loved my mother—in his own way at least. But Alan, my brother, was his whole world. He tried to blame the doctor, but I have been told the poor man could not have done anything, for he was not able to get to the ranch in time. It changed my father. He became tough and savage and vindictive in business matters, even toward old friends. But the change toward me was in the other direction. He began centering his whole life, his business plans for the future, everything, around me. He seemed to want to make up for the way he had treated me."

"A guilty conscience," Lily said.

"I'm afraid so," Ellen replied. "When he knows I am blind he will be capable of anything. Of murder, of an unreasonable desire to strike back at someone—at anything."

"You knew on the train that you were blind, didn't you?" Frank asked. "Why didn't you tell someone at the time?" She did not answer that, so he did it for her. "You kept it a secret because you were afraid he'd kill me then and there. That's the reason, wasn't it?"

Again she refused to answer. Instead, she began to weep heartbrokenly. She covered her face with her hands while emotion racked her slender body. Frank pulled her hands away from her face. "Look at me!" he gritted savagely. "Try to see! Try!"

Lily tried to tear his hands away from the sobbing girl. "Let her alone, Doctah," she screamed, and she was weeping also. "You are torturing her! You are being brutal!"

Frank slowly released Ellen Sloan. He was defeated, utterly beaten. Once more he had hoped that emotional shock would perform the miracle. It had not.

"You don't want to see again," he said. "You don't want to look upon me because you don't want the guilt if your father kills me, because he will blame me for you being blind. That's it, isn't it?"

She did not answer, but he was sure he had found the truth.

They pushed ahead. Lily grasped Frank's hand for a time. "Do not blame Ellen," she whispered. "And, above all, do not try to go to Henry Sloan and tell him how wrong he is, if we live to escape from this place. He must be what you call it—loco?"

The wind moaned around them as though trying malevolently to hold them back. Progress was won at great cost of strength, and only desperation kept them going. However, the Devil Wind was also one great factor in their favor. The blowing sand erased their footprints almost as fast as they were made. Their only guide was Polaris, and it was often obscured by the spume of sand or by the high crests of the dunes around them.

Lily fell, got to her feet, and stumbled ahead, returning to her task of helping Frank guide Ellen Sloan. But she was at the end of her endurance. Frank picked her up in his arms. With Ellen's hand on his shoulder he struggled ahead again. The Chinese girl protested feebly and pleaded to be placed back on her own feet.

"I am strong now, Doctah," she kept insisting. "Very strong. I can keep up with you."

She finally prevailed and managed to fight her way along. But for the guiding star they might have been hopelessly lost in this rolling sea of sand. Even so, to keep doggedly heading south meant climbing the treacherous surfaces of one dune after another. Once a crest was reached, there was before them the sliding descent to the swale at the foot of the next laborious ascent.

Frank called halts often to rest. Weariness was now a drug. He found himself fighting off sleep, even as he forced his legs to keep moving ahead.

The wind began to die and he realized that daybreak was not far away and that they must find a hide-out. The task was baffling. What scant vegetation that found foothold in the scant stretches of open ground not only offered little concealment but would also be no shield against the blast of the sun when the day advanced. The desert was chilly now, but it would be another story in a few more hours. Worse yet, thirst was beginning to gnaw at his throat, and he knew the two girls must be enduring the same pangs.

A bare ridge jutted above a dune that aspired to bury it, offering a possible refuge. They fought their way up the yielding sand until they reached the base of the barren outcrop.

"There is a place," Lily spoke, her voice dry, shrill. "It may do."

It was a crevice between walls of naked rock and it proved big enough to shelter them and deep enough so that they could retreat entirely out of sight. It had another advantage. From that elevation they had a view of their surroundings for some distance.

They huddled in the rocky cleft, and sleep soon claimed them. The predawn chill sharpened its teeth and they clung together, both for warmth and for reassurance that they were still alive and still had hope.

Bright daylight and its warmth awakened Frank. The girls still slept, huddled together in their thin, worn garb. He crawled to the mouth of the slit. The sun was already well up in the sky. The glare from the dunes was almost dazzling, but he could make out a faint, dark line far to the south. The railroad.

He peered in the opposite direction, then sank down. In him arose a savage anger, a primitive urge to rend and kill. This, he knew, must be the reaction of all hunted animals when followed by relentless pursuers.

For he made out black dots along the lower flank of a dune some miles to the north. At that distance he had to watch for many seconds before making sure that they were moving. The dots were horsemen and there were five of them. They were outlaws from the hide-out. They had rounded up mounts and were scouting through the dunes in the hope of picking up the trail of the escaped captives. They must know by this time, beyond doubt, that their quarry was afoot.

Frank scanned the surface of the dune by which he and the girls had mounted to this hide-out and became satisfied that the wind had covered their tracks before it had faded into the dawn calm.

He discovered that he was twirling the cylinder of the six-shooter and that he was thirsting for something more than water. He wanted the chance to pay back those pursuers for their savagery of the past. The iron bands and the lengths of broken chain on his ankles were the measure of their debt to him. These were not men in his calculations, but leeches who would rob and kill and torture as long as they were loose to prey on helpless victims.

The dots were creeping in their direction.

CHAPTER 13

Ellen crept to his side, feeling her way. The metallic clicking of the gun's cylinder had penetrated her slumber. She had long since cast aside the cloth over her eyes. She ran a hand down his arm to the weapon, and that intuitive sense that blindness seemed to be sharpening in her told her of the harsh emotions that were racing in him.

"What is it?" she whispered.

"They're out there," he said. "But they're still a long way north of us. Two miles or more. There's no need to whisper. I count five. They've rounded up horses and are trying to pick up our trail."

"These men are cowards," she said. "They know that you are armed. They will give it up and will turn back."

Lily had joined them, and they lay watching, waiting. Presently Lily spoke. "You are right, Ellen. They are turning back. They have given it up."

The fury drained out of Frank and the weariness returned. More than ever he felt the need for water. He knew the girls were suffering also, but, by unspoken consent, it was a forbidden subject.

"I sighted the railroad a while ago," he said. "But the glare of the sun on the dunes has blotted it out now. But it is too far away to try for it in daytime. In addition, there might be more of those thugs from the hide-out looking for us who haven't quit, and they'd spot us after we got clear of the dunes. We will have to tough it out until dark, then make a try for it."

His tongue was dry, thick, his voice harsh. Ellen came close and ran the tips of her fingers over his unshaven face. "We will do as you say," she said. "You have brought us this far. The Lord will not turn his back on you now."

"Of course," he said, but he was thinking of the day-long ordeal they faced without water, not to mention the march at night that lay ahead of them.

"You need a shave," Ellen said. "Lily tells me that under that thicket of whiskers is a very good-looking man."

"The Chinese are a very polite people," he said. "I wouldn't want to disillusion you. I may never shave again so as to keep the truth from you."

"You are telling me that I will see again," she said. "You seem to be sure of it."

"I'm sure," he said. "And you must be sure too."

"Look!" Lily exclaimed, pointing. "Am I imagining it? I thought I saw more riders. I do not see them now. But I *did* see them. They are far away, to the east, but they seemed to be coming from the direction of the railroad."

They waited, straining their eyes. For a long time they saw nothing but the increasing shimmer of the sand in the sun. Then Frank spoke. "There they are!"

They were tiny specks among the great dunes east of them, but their general route appeared to be north. The outlaw oasis lay in that direction.

Frank counted the numbers aloud. "Four. Only two are riders. Two pack animals."

"The Haskells," Lily said. "I did not believe them when they told the others they would come back. But I was wrong."

"It's my guess they've got the ransom," Frank said. "It's my guess also that they've cached it somewhere, or will do so, and will go back to the hide-out with some yarn that Henry Sloan has demanded more evidence that Ellen is still in their hands. Then they plan to ask for more ransom."

The small figures vanished among the dunes, reappeared, vanished. Finally they were close enough to verify identification. "It's the Haskells all right," Frank said. "They must have got back to the dunes while the wind was still blowing so as to cover their trail, then camped awhile to spell the horses. Now they could be back in the hide-out before dark. The mules are carrying water bags that look like they're still in good shape. They must have filled up last night somewhere, likely at the ranch of this Steve who handles the blinker on the railroad end."

He saw that the route the Haskells were following apparently would take them less than a mile from the point where he and the girls crouched, watching. Presently they vanished beyond a great, serpentine-shaped dune that angled northward.

Frank arose. "Stay here," he said. "In case I don't come back, wait until dark, then try to make it to the railroad."

"No." Both girls again spoke almost in one voice. They clasped hands in the gesture of unity he was beginning to expect from them. "We do not part now," Ellen went on. "We believe we know what you intend to try to do."

Frank rattled the broken chain of the bands that tortured his ankles. "Bart Haskell has the key to these things," he said. "That's one plan that I have."

"You are going to fight them," Ellen said. "With guns."

"I've got one advantage," he said. "And it may be a big one. They don't know we are around. They don't know we escaped. Otherwise they'd be looking for us, trying to keep to cover. It's my guess they can't see the ridge where they do the heliographing, even if Whitey is up there."

Knowing it was useless to continue insisting that they

part from him, he took Ellen's hand and led the way. They left the rocky outcrop and slogged down the sandy face of the dune to the swale. There they faced the huge dune beyond which Frank hoped the Haskells were still traveling. He set as fast a pace as he dared in the impeding sand.

The thirst was now malevolently upon them. The Indians of the desert had a name for it. Translated into white men's talk it meant "the strong thirst."

"There is water on the pack mules," he said to the girls. That thought was their strength, their goal, their chance for life, now that they were committed to this course.

The serpentine dune curved to the left, then to the right. Frank was attempting to estimate distances, hoping that they were paralleling the route of the Haskells beyond the great comber of sand. There was always the chance that the quarry might have swerved in some other direction. If so, Frank knew that the chase was hopeless. He refused to mention that possibility. If Ellen and Lily shared that fear, they also kept it to themselves, but they all knew the extent of the gamble they were risking. The strength they were expending in this effort could never be recovered without help. And help meant water.

Frank made his decision. "Up," he said, and he led the way up the yielding face of the dune. He saw the strained faces of the girls. They were almost on hands and knees, clawing at the sand for progress, looking toward the crest that seemed so unattainable.

But they reached it. For a space they lay utterly spent, with the bitter sun beating down on them. Then Frank crawled a few feet ahead and cautiously peered over the crest. He was risking failure, for he knew that any foreign object was easy to detect in this white sea. The sand was slightly crusted here and he could not wallow into it. He was forced to rise to his knees.

The dune on this lee side dropped almost perpendicularly to a swale. The Haskells were halted there. Evidently they had been leading their horses and mules through heavy, clinging sand and they were now adjusting nose bags to water the animals. Their backs were turned and they were unaware that Frank was peering down at them from the summit of the great dune.

CHAPTER 14

The Haskells finished caring for the livestock, then used tin cups to drink from one of the water bags. They were talking and peering around as though in search of something. At first Frank believed they might have sighted danger of some kind. Bart Haskell was pointing ahead. The dune curved westward just ahead, and Frank could see barren rock and ledges that evidently were kept free of the creeping waves of sand by some freak of the wind.

The Haskells walked ahead, investigating the boulders. They peered around and seemed to be picking out landmarks, pacing off distances. Suddenly Frank guessed their purpose. He sank back out of sight as the pair started to retrace their steps.

He waited breathlessly for many seconds before chancing another look. He had been right. The Haskells were lifting two weighted canvas bags off the pack mules. These they carried up the swale into the barren ground and pushed them into a crevice beneath a large boulder that easily stood as a landmark. Small rocks and brush were carefully piled over the cache.

The pair returned to the livestock and were obviously preparing to mount and head away. The girls were crawling to Frank's side. He waved them back, then leaped over the crest, the revolver in his hand.

He landed on the steep slope of sand, digging his heels. The sand was powder-dry and loose. Instantly he was riding an avalanche. The Haskells, whose attitudes had been those of men well satisfied with themselves and in no danger, turned, looking up.

They were too late. The avalanche, with Frank on its face, was upon them. Clem uttered a squawk of fear. He tried to run, tried to draw his six-shooter, but was not quick enough. The billow of sand overtook him, burying him to his armpits. He wrested his arms clear and began hysterically clawing at the sand, but his efforts only drove him deeper until only his head was clear.

Bart was tougher. He screeched an oath, and managed to draw and get off one shot in Frank's direction, but it went far from the mark, for he was running to escape the onrush of sand. He might have made it, but he tripped and went down. An instant later he was engulfed by the avalanche. He fought his way clear, but when he looked up, gasping and choking, he was facing the muzzle of Frank's pistol.

"Go ahead, Bart," Frank said. "Give me a good excuse. You're a man who kidnaps girls, slaps them around, milks a father of everything you can squeeze out of him. Then you aim to murder the girls and me. You've got a gun in your hand. Lift it and you won't live to be hung. Or drop it."

Bart Haskell let the weapon fall from his fingers. He lifted his arms. "Don't kill me, Doc," he croaked.

The two girls arrived, having descended from the dune by a route safer than Frank's choice. Between them they dragged Clem out of the sand, and Frank disarmed him. Clem, dazed, was gagging and spent.

The avalanche of sand had knocked one of the saddle horses off its feet and buried the other horse and the two mules to their bellies, but they were all struggling free. The downed animal regained its feet and seemed unhurt. It and its companions stood trembling, wild-eyed, reins and lead ropes dangling.

Frank made sure the action on both of the seized pistols was working. He handed one of the guns to Lily, unloaded the other, and hung it on one of the pack mules.

"Do you know how to shoot that thing?" he asked Lily.

"Yes—yes!" she quavered.

"Use both hands," he told her. "Shoot if I tell you, but be damned sure it's them you hit and not me."

"What can I do?" Ellen demanded. "Exactly what has happened?"

"The doctah descended on them from the sky and buried them in the sand," Lily explained. Her quavering voice firmed and she even tried to laugh, although it was not much of a success. "We have the two. The fathah and son who were so mean to us. Yes, we have them."

Frank searched Bart until he found the key that freed him from the ankle bands. He clamped the bands on Bart's ankles, winding the metal tight. "So you'll know how it feels, Bart," he said.

"Give me the knife," he said to Lily.

She hesitated, turning to Ellen. "What will you do with it, Doctor?" Ellen asked. "I am the one who has it."

"For God's sake!" Frank exploded. "I need it to cut some ropes to tie up their hands. Give me the kife. Oh, I'll give it back to you if it's that important. But you'll never need it again, now will you?"

She had contrived a thong by which she had hung the knife about her throat and had sheathed it in a makeshift cloth scabbard so that it could be carried out of sight in the bosom of her blouse. She handed it to him and he used it to cut thongs from the lead ropes and saddle strings with which he lashed the hands of the two prisoners at their backs. He hesitated, then reluctantly placed the knife back in her hand.

The Haskells were still stunned, stricken by what had happened to them. The fear of the hang rope was upon them.

One of the sizable water bags on a mule was still well filled. Frank said to Lily, "You first," and drew her to the spout. She crouched, letting the precious water end the torture of her parched tongue and throat. He and Ellen drank, and new life returned to them.

"What are you goin' to do with us?" Bart Haskell asked hoarsely.

"Take you in so that you can be hung proper," Frank said.

"What if we gave you enough money to set you up on easy street for a long time to come?" Bart asked.

Frank walked down the swale to the cache, kicked aside the rocks and brush that had been placed for concealment, and dragged out the weighted canvas bags. He freed the drawstring of one and peered. It contained twenty-dollar gold pieces. He shouldered the bags and returned.

"Is this the money you were talking about, Bart?" he asked.

Bart Haskell did not answer. Frank scouted the open area and found an overhang on a ledge that would at least offer some shelter from the sun. He prodded the Haskells ahead of them while he and Lily led the horses and pack animals. He shoved the Haskells into the shelter and bound their ankles.

"We'll wait until toward sundown to travel," he told the girls. We can make it to the railroad long before midnight now that we've got water. I'll stand first watch. Lily can spell me after she gets some sleep."

Utter exhaustion was bearing down on all of them, now

that tension was easing. Frank could see that the two girls had passed their physical reserve and were in a state of collapse. They fell asleep the instant they huddled together. He fought the desire to do the same, for the Haskells were watching every move, waiting a chance to test the bonds, of whose strength Frank was none too sure.

Lily awakened after two hours, and insisted on taking over. She had the six-shooter in her hand, and there was in her the determination to shoot if necessary. The Haskells must have recognized that, for they had made no move to challenge that strength of will in her by the time Frank awakened.

The afternoon heat, reflected by the walls, was almost intolerable, but there was more water on the second mule and that carried them through. When the sun was touching the last spires of the ridges, Frank gave the word to move out.

He gave water sparingly to the livestock and the humans. He freed the ankles of Clem, but kept the elder man impeded by shackles and the dragging chains, then prodded them to their feet.

He loaded the bags of coin on the mules. "We'll all have to walk for a while down the draw," he said. "The sand is too heavy and the horses would mire. When we reach better going, Ellen will ride Clem's horse and I'll take Bart's. Lily, darling, you'll have a mule as a steed, for they say you don't weigh more than a cup of tea. You'll have a water bag and a sack of gold to keep you company."

"What about us?" Bart Haskell demanded.

"You've got two legs, Bart," Frank said. "So has Clem."

"How fur you goin' to make us walk?" Haskell moaned.

"To the railroad."

"What? Thet's well onto ten miles, man. Air you aimin' on killin' us?"

"No such luck," Frank said. "Let's get moving."

He shoved the Haskells ahead of him. Ellen placed a hand on his arm for guidance, and he led the two saddle animals, with Lily bringing up the rear with the mules.

They had hard going, especially through the sand Frank had brought down in his avalanche, with the animals floundering and trying to rebel. The last rays of the setting sun were striking the flanks of the dunes around them.

Lily and the mules had fallen a hundred yards or more behind them, but was motioning that she needed no help, when Frank rounded a turn in the draw. And there, confronting them, stood three men. One was a Piute Indian, wearing only a breechclout, moccasins, and a beaded band to hold back his thick black hair. He was wiry and up in years and the sun had baked his brown skin almost black. Frank knew him. He was a subchief who had been called on often to help law officers trail criminals or to seek lost prospectors in the desert. Evidently he had, at last, been induced to lead the way into the Playground.

Accompanying the Piute were two white men. One was a wiry, gaunt man burned almost as dark as the Indian. He had a deputy's star pinned to his shirt and packed a gun in a holster. He was Bill Hubbard, a tough, desert-wise deputy sheriff who was usually stationed at Barstow.

Frank knew the other white man also. This one was Henry Sloan. The rancher looked old, exhausted. Even his Panama hat seemed to droop tiredly over the face of a man who had driven himself and others to the limit.

Henry Sloan halted. He was a dozen yards ahead of the deputy. He stood there, crouching slowly. His haggard eyes flicked from the Haskells to his daughter. And then to Frank. For a space there was no sound. The Indian trailer and Bill Hubbard had halted also.

"What is it?" Ellen spoke sharply, breaking the silence.

"It's your father," Frank said. "He's found us. He's with

a Piute trailer named Little Fox. There's another man. We—"

Henry Sloan spoke hoarsely. "I was right. You *were* in on it, Conroy, if that's really your name. I told you I would kill you on sight."

Henry Sloan was drawing the pistol he carried thrust in his belt. He meant to shoot.

Frank could understand the rancher's error. Lily and the mules had not yet come in sight. Henry Sloan had not realized that the Haskells were prisoners. All that he was seeing was his daughter in the hands of the men who had kidnaped her and had collected ransom. And Frank was with them.

Ellen uttered a wild scream. She groped for Frank and twisted her own body in front of him as a shield just as her father fired.

Frank heard the impact of the bullet. The force of it drove her back against him so violently that both of them fell. For an instant he lay there with her in his arms. He had the empty, lost sensation of complete futility, of a purposeless life. He believed she had taken the bullet in her heart.

He lifted her limp body clear, got to his knees, and drew the six-shooter. Henry Sloan was standing there, the smoke of the exploded cartridge drifting above his head. He was staring at his daughter, stunned, horrified.

Frank rocked back the hammer on his weapon. "You've killed her," he said numbly. "You don't deserve to live."

Ellen spoke faintly. "No! No! Not that, above all! Not that!"

She groped for his arm, pulled the six-shooter down. She seemed to be looking up at him. In her face was supplication, and desperation. But, above all, tenderness.

"You can see?" he asked hoarsely.

"Does it matter?" she replied. "We are still together."

Lily arrived, talking incoherently. Frank stripped away the blouse Ellen was wearing, a blouse that was stained with blood.

After a moment he looked at Lily. "Thank God!" he said humbly.

The bullet had struck the wide blade of the knife that Ellen had carried in its sheath over her breast. The metal had deflected the slug. It had gouged a minor injury. The impact had caused the principal damage, but Frank began to be sure there was no permanent effect Ellen was already emerging from the shock of the blow.

Henry Sloan had lowered his pistol. Bill Hubbard came out of his trance, moved up, and took the weapon from the rancher's hand.

Henry Sloan, horror still in his face, came stumbling to his daughter's side. He looked at Frank. "Is she—is she—?" he began.

"You failed to kill her this time," Frank said. "Or me."

More men appeared. They were armed, and leading horses in the soft underfooting. There were nearly a score of them, all obviously hand-picked desert men, some wearing the badges of deputies. Ramon Zapata was with them, and he came striding to stand by Frank. "I did not expect to ever see you alive again, amigo," he said. "I am very glad."

The posse was equipped with a pack train carrying ample water, and had also brought Joel Russell, Frank's doctor friend from San Bernardino. He helped Frank treat Ellen. She kept clinging to Frank's hand, kept saying, "My dear! My dear! I *do* want to see you."

Frank bent and kissed her. "You will," he said. "I'll do the seeing for both of us if need be. I will never leave you."

Lily wept great tears of joy. "You *will* see again, Ellen," G she sobbed. "You will be so happy, you and the doctah. I have known that you had come to love him and that he loves you."

Among the posse was a young broad-shouldered Chinese coolie. He shyly drew Lily to his side. "Your brothah is in a hospital in San Bernardino, Lily," he said. "He will soon be well. I am happy that you are safe. Very, very happy. I prayed to our ancestors that this would be so."

She clung to him with the tenderness of a woman in love who had been restored to a future she had felt was lost.

Frank lifted Ellen to her feet. "Lean on me," he said.

"Yes," she said. "Oh yes. I will always lean on you."

Joel Russell looked questioningly at Frank. "She can't see," Frank said. "I believe it's only a temporary nerve paralysis. I will take her to San Francisco to see Elias Burke."

"Of course," Russell said. "Burke is a genius at that sort of thing."

Around them the posse was preparing to continue on into the Devil's Playground to clean out the nest of ruffians.

Henry Sloan stood helpless and alone in the background. His daughter spoke. "Father, where are you? Come with us. It was all a mistake, a nightmare. But it's over now."

Henry Sloan, as though reprieved from the tomb, came toward his daughter and Frank to join them.

Cliff Farrell was born in Zanesville, Ohio, where earlier Zane Grey had been born. Following graduation from high school, Farrell became a newspaper reporter. Over the next decade he worked his way west by means of a string of newspaper jobs and for thirty-one years was employed, mostly as sports editor, for the *Los Angeles Examiner.* He would later claim that he began writing for pulp magazines because he grew bored with journalism. His first Western stories were written for *Cowboy Stories* in 1926 and his byline was A. Clifford Farrell. By 1928 this byline was abbreviated to Cliff Farrell, and this it remained for the rest of his career. In 1933 Farrell was invited to contribute a story for the first issue of *Dime Western.* He soon became a regular contributor to this magazine and to *Star Western* as well. In fact, many months he would have a short novel in both magazines. Farrell became such a staple at Popular Publications that by the end of the 1930s he was contributing as much as 400,000 words a year to their various Western magazines. In all, Farrell wrote nearly 600 stories for the magazine market. His earliest Western fiction tended to stress action and gun play, but increasingly his stories began to focus on characters in historical situations and the problems faced by those characters. *Follow the New Grass* (1954) was Farrell's first Western novel, a story concerned with a desperate battle over grazing rights in the Cheyenne Indian reserve. It was followed by *West with the Missouri* (1955), an exciting story of riverboats, gamblers, and gunmen. *Fort Deception* (1960), *Ride the Wild Country* (1963), *The Renegade* (1970), and *The Devil's Playground* (1976) are among the best of Farrell's later Western novels. *Desperate Journey,* a first collection of Cliff Farrell's Western short stories, has also been published.